"This is my city and my home, and you are the _____. There is to be a _____ my story, not _____ reaching o_____ tendril of _____acher's cheek.

He felt carnal and hungry. Desire ran hot in his veins.

"The only story is the truth. You have a nephew you refuse to acknowledge, never mind support."

"But is he my nephew?"

"Yes, you know he is. I've sent you the birth certificate and we can do a DNA test while I'm here—"

"Proving what?" he retorted. Before she could answer, he reached for her again, his hand coiling in her long dark hair, tilting her head back to take her mouth in a long, searing kiss.

She didn't stiffen or resist. If anything, she leaned into him, and he wrapped an arm around her slender frame, holding her against him as he deepened the kiss, his tongue sweeping her mouth, tasting her, weakening her defenses. By the time he lifted his head, she was silent, no fight left in her. Her wide brown eyes looked up into his.

"You should never underestimate your opponent, Rachel," he said quietly, running his thumb lightly across her soft flushed cheek. "And you most definitely shouldn't have underestimated me."

Conveniently Wed!

Conveniently wedded, passionately bedded!

Whether there's a debt to be paid,
a will to be obeyed or a business to be saved...
she's got no choice but to say, "I do!"

But these billionaire bridegrooms have got
another think coming if they think marriage will be
that easy...

Soon their convenient brides become the objects
of an *inconvenient* desire!

Look out for these Conveniently Wed! stories

Bought with the Italian's Ring by Tara Pammi

Bound to the Sicilian's Bed by Sharon Kendrick

Imprisoned by the Greek's Ring by Caitlin Crews

Coming soon!

Jane Porter

HIS MERCILESS MARRIAGE BARGAIN

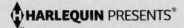

HARLEQUIN PRESENTS®

Recycling programs
for this product may
not exist in your area.

ISBN-13: 978-1-335-50402-9

His Merciless Marriage Bargain

First North American publication 2017

Copyright © 2017 by Jane Porter

This edition published by arrangement with Harlequin Books S.A.

For questions and comments about the quality of this book,
please contact us at CustomerService@Harlequin.com.

Printed in U.S.A.

New York Times and *USA TODAY* bestselling author **Jane Porter** has written forty romances and eleven women's fiction novels since her first sale to Harlequin in 2000. A five-time RITA® Award finalist, Jane is known for her passionate, emotional and sensual novels, and loves nothing more than alpha heroes, exotic locations and happily-ever-afters. Today Jane lives in sunny San Clemente, California, with her surfer husband and three sons. Visit janeporter.com.

CHAPTER ONE

RACHEL BERN STOOD outside the imposing doors of the Palazzo Marcello shivering, the wind grabbing at her black coat and ponytail, sending both flying.

Overhead, thick gray clouds blanketed the sky and the rising tides sent water surging over the banks of the lagoon, wetting the streets of Venice, but the stormy weather wasn't so different from her weather in Seattle. She'd grown up with rain and damp. This morning she wasn't shivering from cold, but nerves.

This could go so very wrong. It could blow up in her face, leaving her and Michael in an even worse situation, but she was at her wit's end. If this didn't get Giovanni Marcello's attention, nothing would. She'd tried everything else, tried every other form of communication, but every attempt resulted in silence and the silence was destructive. Crushing. She was taking a huge risk, but what else could she do?

Giovanni Marcello, an Italian billionaire, was also one of the most reclusive businessmen in

Italy. He rarely socialized. He had no direct email or phone, and when Rachel finally reached Signor Marcello's front office management, they were noncommittal about relaying messages to the CEO of the holding company, Marcello SpA. And so she was here, at the Palazzo Marcello in Venice, the family's home for the past two hundred years. Until the turn of the twentieth century, the Marcellos had been a shrewd, successful manufacturing family that had earned its place in society through hard work and wealth, but in the past forty years, the family had expanded from manufacturing and construction into real estate and, under the helm of Giovanni Marcello, investing in world markets. The Marcello fortune had quadrupled through Giovanni's management, and they had become one of the most powerful and influential families in Italy.

Thirty-eight-year-old Giovanni continued to head up the holding company based in Rome, but she'd just discovered through her hired investigator that he rarely put in an appearance at the office, choosing instead to work from Venice. Which was why she was now here on his doorstep, exhausted and jet-lagged from traveling with a six-month-old baby, but determined. He couldn't ignore her any longer. There would be no more shutting her out, or more importantly, Michael.

Heart aching, eyes stinging, she glanced down at the bundle in her arms, the baby thankfully finally sleeping, and silently apologized for what she was about to do. "It's for your sake," she whispered, bringing him close to her chest and giving a light squeeze. "And I'm not going far, I promise."

Even in his sleep, the baby wriggled in protest. She smiled ruefully, easing her hold, but she couldn't ease the guilt. She hadn't slept since they left Seattle, but then, she hadn't slept in months, not since she'd become his full-time caregiver. At six months he should be ready to sleep through the night, but maybe he felt how unsettled she was, or maybe he was missing his mother...

Rachel's eyes stung and her heart smarted. If only she'd done more for Juliet after Michael's birth, if only she'd understood how distraught she had been...

But Rachel couldn't turn back time, and so she was here, about to hand him over to his father's family. Not forever, of course, just for a few minutes, but to make a point. They needed help. She was broke and about to lose her job, and it wasn't right, not when his father's family could, and should, help.

Swallowing, she raised her hand and knocked firmly on the door, and then, in case the knock couldn't be heard inside, she pressed the button for the doorbell mounted on the wall. Did the bell even work, she wondered? Had anyone heard her?

Between the wind and the lapping of water and the voices of tourists and travelers on the lagoon, she wasn't sure if anyone was stirring within the palazzo. She knew she was being watched, though, and not from within the building, but from the photographers stationed outside. There was one across the lagoon and another on a balcony of an adjacent building, as well as another parked in a tethered gondola. She'd seen the cameras as she stepped off the water taxi and was glad to see them as she'd been the one to tip them off, teasing the various media outlets that something significant was happening today, something to do with a Marcello baby.

It was easy enough to accomplish when one's job hinged on publicity, marketing and customer relations for AeroDynamics, one of the largest airline manufacturers in the world. Normally her PR efforts were to attract new, affluent customers—sheikhs, tycoons, sports figures, celebrities—by showcasing AeroDynamics sleek jet designs and luxurious interiors, but today she needed the media because they could apply pressure for her. Their photos would draw attention, and subsequent public scrutiny, and Giovanni Marcello would not like it. He valued his privacy and would take immediate steps to curtail the attention. But before he did that, she needed to make sure that she got the right action and the proper results. She didn't want to shame the Marcellos, or alienate them. She needed them on her side—correction, on Michael's side—but her actions now might do the opposite and push them further away—

No, she couldn't go there. She wouldn't think that way. Giovanni Marcello had to accept Michael, and he would, once he saw how much his nephew looked like his brother.

Rachel lifted her hand to knock again, but the door swung open before she could rap a second time. A tall thin elderly man stood in the doorway. Shadows stretched behind him. From the doorstep, the space appeared cavernous, with a glinting of an ornate chandelier high overhead.

She looked from the grand light fixture to the elderly man. He wore a plain dark suit, a very simple suit, and she suspected he wasn't family, but someone who worked for the Marcellos. "Signor Marcello, *per favore*," she said calmly, crisply, praying her Italian would be understood. She'd practiced the phrase on the flight, repeating the simple request over and over to ensure she could deliver the words with the right note of authority.

"*Signor Marcello non è disponibile,*" he answered flatly.

Her brows furrowed as she tried to decipher what he'd said. *Non* was not. *Disponibile* could mean just about anything but she sensed it was a negative, either way.

"*È lui non a casa?*" she stumbled, struggling to remember the words, not at all sure she was getting the tense right, or the correct words, never mind the words in the proper order. Her little phrase book only gave her so many options.

"No. Addio."

She understood those words. *No,* and *goodbye.*

She moved forward swiftly before he could close the door on her, using her low-heeled boot to keep the door ajar.

"Il bambino Michael Marcello," she said in Italian, before switching to English as she thrust the infant into the old man's arms. "Please tell Signor Marcello that Michael will need a bottle when he wakes."

She drew the diaper bag strap from her shoulder and set the bulging bag down on the doorstep at the man's feet. "He will also need a diaper change, probably before the bottle," she added, fighting to keep her voice even, almost impossible when her heart raced and she already itched to reach out and wrench the baby back. "Everything he needs is in the bag, including his schedule to help him adjust. If there are questions, my hotel information is in the bag, along with my cell number."

And then her voice did break and her throat sealed closed and she turned away, walking quickly before the tears could fall.

It's for Michael, she told herself, swiping tears as she hurried toward the canal. *Be brave. Be strong. You're doing this for him.*

The baby wouldn't be away from her for more

than a few minutes because she fully expected
Giovanni Marcello to come after her. If not now,
then surely at her hotel, which was less than five
minutes away by water taxi, as she'd left all her
contact details in the diaper bag.

And yet, every step she took carried her farther from the palazzo and closer to the water taxi
waiting for her, and now with Michael out of her
arms, she felt hollow and empty, every instinct in
her screaming for her to turn around and go back
and have this out with Giovanni, face-to-face.

But what if Giovanni refused to come to the
door? How was she to force Giovanni out for the
necessary conversation?

The old man shouted something, his voice thin
and sharp. She didn't understand, but one word
did stand out. *Polizia.* Was he threatening to call
the police? She wasn't surprised if he was. It's
what she'd do if someone just abandoned a six-
month-old infant to her care. Numb and heartsick,
she kept her focus on the water taxi tethered in
the canal. The driver was watching her and she
waved, signaling that she was ready to go.

Seconds later, a hand seized her upper arm.
The fingers gripped her tightly, the hold pain-
ful. "Ouch!" Rachel winced at the painful hold.
"Let go."

"Stop running," the deep male voice ground
out, the voice as hard as the punishing grip, his
English perfect with just the slightest accent.

She turned around, the persistent wind having loosened dark strands from her ponytail, making it hard to see him through the tangle of hair. "I'm not running," she said fiercely, trying to free herself, but he stood close, his grip unrelenting. "Can you give me some space, please?"

"Not a chance, Miss Bern."

She knew then who this tall man was, and a shiver raced through her as she pushed long strands of hair behind her ears. Giovanni Marcello wasn't just tall, he was impressively broad through the shoulders, with thick black hair, light eyes and high cheekbones above a firm, unsmiling mouth. She'd seen pictures of him on the internet. There weren't many, as he didn't attend a lot of social events like his brother Antonio had, but in every photo he was elegantly dressed, impeccably groomed. Polished. Gleaming. Hard.

He looked even harder in person. His light eyes—an icy blue—glittered down at her and his strong, chiseled features were set. Grim.

She felt a flutter of fear. It crossed her mind that beneath the groomed exterior was something dark and brooding, something that struck her as not entirely civilized.

Rachel took a step back, needing her distance even more now.

"You said you weren't running," he growled.

"I'm not going anywhere, and there's no need for you to be on top of me."

"Are you unwell, Miss Bern? Are you having a breakdown?"

"Why would you ask that?"

"Because you've just abandoned a child on my doorstep."

"He's not being abandoned. You're his uncle."

"I strongly suggest you retrieve the child before the police arrive."

"Let the police come. At least then the world will know the truth."

He arched a black brow. "So you *are* unwell."

"I'm perfectly well. In fact, I couldn't be better. You have no idea how difficult it has been to locate you. Months of investigation, not to mention money I couldn't afford to spend on a private investigator, but at least we are here now, face-to-face, ready to discuss new responsibilities."

"The only thing I have to say to you is collect the child—"

"Your nephew."

"And return home before this becomes unpleasant for everybody."

"It's already unpleasant for me. Your help is desperately needed."

"You, and he, are not my problem."

"Michael is a Marcello. He's your late brother's only child, and he should be protected and provided for by his family."

"That is not going to happen."

"I think it will."

His eyes narrowed, the icy blue irises partially hidden by dense black lashes. "You are deliberately trying to provoke me."

"And why not? You've done nothing but irritate and provoke me for the past few months. You had many opportunities to reply to my emails and phone calls, but you couldn't be bothered to reach out, so now I'm returning to you what is yours." Which wasn't actually true—she wasn't leaving Michael here, but she didn't have to let him know that.

"You're definitely not sound if you're abandoning your sister's son—"

"And Antonio's," she interrupted tautly. "If you recall your lessons in biology, conception requires a sperm and an egg, and in this instance it's Juliet's and Antonio's—" She paused, grinding down to hold back the rest of the hot painful words, words that ached and kept her from sleeping and eating. Juliet had always been foolish and impractical, her dreams littered with hearts, flowers, expensive sports cars and wealthy boyfriends. "The DNA paperwork is inside his diaper bag," she continued. "You'll find his medical records and everything you need to know about his routine in there, too. I've done my part. Now it's your turn." She gave him a brittle nod and turned away, grateful for the water taxi that still waited for her.

He caught her once more, this time by the nape,

warm fingers sliding beneath her ponytail to wrap around her neck. "You're going nowhere, Miss Bern, at least not without that child." His voice had dropped, deepening, and she shuddered at the sensation burning through her.

His grip was in no way painful but her skin tingled from head to toe. It was almost as if he'd plugged her into an electric socket. As he turned her to face him, goose bumps covered her arms, and every part of her felt unbearably sensitive.

She looked up into his cool blue eyes and went hot, then cold, feeling a frisson of awareness streak through her. She wasn't afraid, but the sensation was too sharp, too intense to be pleasurable. "And you really must stop manhandling me, Signor Marcello," she answered faintly, her heart thudding violently.

"Why is that, Miss Bern?"

She stared up into his face, her gaze locking with his. There was nothing icy about his eyes now. No, they glowed with intelligence and heat and power. There was a physicality about him that stole her breath, knocking her off balance. She tried to gather her thoughts but his energy was so strong she felt it hum through her, lighting her up, making her feel as if he'd somehow stripped her bare.

Gulping for air, she looked down at his strong straight nose and the brackets on either side of his mouth. His face was not a boy's but a man's, with creases and lines, and if she didn't dislike him so much, she would have found the creases beautiful. "You are giving the paparazzi quite a show, you know," she whispered.

His strong black brows pulled.

"All the manhandling won't look well in tomorrow's papers. I'm afraid there are too many incriminating photos."

"Incriminating photos—" He broke off abruptly, understanding dawning.

His hand dropped even as his gaze scanned the wide canal and the narrow pavement fronting the water and old buildings. She saw the moment he spotted the first of the cameras, and then others. His dark head turned, his gaze raking her, the blue fire blistering her. "What have you done?"

His voice was deep and rough, his accent more pronounced. Her pulse drummed and her insides churned. She'd scored her first hit, and it scared her. She wasn't accustomed to battling anyone, much less a powerful man. In her work, she assisted, providing support and information. She didn't challenge or contradict.

"I did what needed to be done," she said hoarsely. "You refused to acknowledge your nephew. Your family falls in step with whatever you say, and so I've pressed the issue. Now the whole world knows that your brother's son has been returned to your family."

* * *

Giovanni Marcello drew a slow deep breath and then another. He was shocked as well as livid. He'd been played. *Played.* By a manipulative, money-hungry American no less. He despised gold diggers. Greedy, selfish, soulless. "You contacted the media, inviting them here today?"

"I did."

Rachel was no different from her sister. His fingers curled a little, the only sign that he was seething inwardly. "You're pleased with yourself."

"I'm pleased that you've been forced out of hiding—"

"I was never hiding. Everyone knows this is my home. It's common knowledge that I work here, as well."

"Then why is this the first time I've had a conversation with you? I've reached out to your company staff again and again, and you've never bothered to respond to anything!"

Who was she to demand anything from him? From the start her family had only wanted one thing: to milk the Marcellos. Her sister, Juliet Bern, wasn't in love with his brother, rather she wanted Antonio's money. And once she could no longer blackmail Antonio, Juliet turned on his family, and then once Juliet was gone, it was Rachel's turn. Disgusting. "I owe you nothing, and my family owes you nothing. Your sister is gone. Well, my brother is gone, too. Such is life—"

"Juliet said you had a heart of ice."

"Do you really think you're the first woman to try to entrap Antonio?" *Or me?* Gio silently added, as he'd been played for a fool once, but he'd learned. He knew better than to trust a pretty face.

"I didn't entrap anyone. I didn't sleep with anyone. I find no pleasure in this, Signor Marcello. If anything, I'm horrified. I am not reckless. I do not fall in love with strangers, or make love to handsome wealthy Italian men. I have scruples and morals, and you are not someone I admire, and your wealth doesn't make you appealing. Your wealth, though, can help a little boy who needs support."

"So I'm to applaud you?"

"*No.* Just have a conscience, please."

From the corner of his eye, Giovanni saw a photographer move, crouching as he crept forward, snapping away. His gut tightened, his chest hot with barely leashed anger.

He couldn't believe she'd managed to draw him out of the palazzo and into this scene, a very public scene with witnesses everywhere.

With his position at the helm of the family business, he'd worked hard to keep personal affairs out of the news. It'd taken nearly a decade to restore his family's fortune and his family's reputation, but finally the Marcellos were a name to be proud of and a brand that garnered respect. It hadn't been easy to redeem their name, but he'd managed it through consistent, focused effort. Now, in one reckless moment, this American was about to turn the Marcellos into tabloid fodder once more.

He wasn't ready. He was still struggling to come to terms with his brother's death and refused to have Antonio's memory darkened, his name besmirched, by those consumed with greed. "This isn't a conversation I intend to continue on the streets of Venice," he ground out. He was usually so good at avoiding confrontations. He knew how to manage conflict. And yet here they were, staging an epic soap opera, just a block off the Grand Canal. It couldn't be more public. "Nor am I about to let you abuse my family. If there is to be a story, I shall provide the story, not you."

"It's a little late for that, Signor Marcello. The story has been captured on a half-dozen different cameras. I guarantee within the hour you'll find those images online. Tabloids pay—"

"I'm fully aware of how the paparazzi works."

"Then you're also aware of what they have to work with—me handing the baby to your employee, you chasing after me and now us arguing in front of my water taxi." She paused. "Wouldn't it have been so much easier to have just taken my phone call?"

His gaze swept her face. He felt an uneasy memory of another woman who looked very much like this American Rachel Bern…

Another beautiful brunette who had been exquisitely confident...

He pushed the memory of his fiancée, Adelisa, from mind, but her memory served a purpose. It reminded him of his vow that he'd never let a woman have the upper hand again. Fortunately, he knew that stories could be massaged, and facts weren't always objective. Rachel had come to give the photographers a fantastic shot, something they could take to every newspaper and magazine, and Gio could help her with that. He could ensure the paparazzi photographers with their telephoto lenses had something significant to capture, something that would derail her strategy.

Giovanni pulled her to him, one arm locking around her waist, the other hand free to lift her face. Holding her captive, he cupped her chin and jaw, angling her face up to his. He saw a flare of panic in her eyes, the brown irises shot with flecks of green and gold, before he dropped his head, capturing her mouth with his.

She stiffened, her lips still, her breath bottling. He could feel her fear and tension and he instantly gentled the kiss. Although he'd reached for her in anger, he wasn't in the habit of kissing a woman in anger.

Her mouth was soft and warm. Despite her tension, she was soft and warm and he pulled her closer, tipping her head farther back to tease her lips. He stroked the seam with the tip of his tongue, her mouth generous and pliant. A quiver raced through her, her body shuddering against him and he stroked the seam again, playing with the full upper lip, catching the bow gently in his teeth.

She made a hoarse sound, not in pain, but pleasure, and a lance of hot desire streaked through him, making him hard all over.

He deepened the kiss, her lips parting for him, giving him access to the sweet heat of her mouth. It had been months since he'd enjoyed a kiss half so much, and he took his time, the kiss an exploration of taste and texture and response. His tongue traced the edge of her upper lip and he felt her shudder, her mouth opening wider.

She tasted sweet and hot, but also surprisingly innocent, and his body throbbed, blood drumming in his veins. With his arm in the small of her back, he pulled her even closer, stroking her mouth, over her lower lip, and then finding her tongue, making her shiver again.

Her breathless sighs and little shivers whetted his appetite. It'd been a long time since he felt hunger like this. It had been a year and a half since he'd broken things off with his last mistress, and he'd spent evenings with different women since, but he hadn't slept with any of them. How could he when there was no desire? Antonio's death had numbed him to everything, until now.

Abruptly Gio released Rachel and took a step back, his pulse thudding hard and heavy, echoing the hot ache in his groin. She stood dazed and motionless, her brown eyes cloudy and bemused.

"That should give your photographer friends something intriguing to sell." His voice sounded harsh even to his own ears. "It will be interesting to see what story the papers run with the addition of these news shots. Is it really about the baby? Or is this more? A lover's quarrel, their passionate encounter, an emotional goodbye?"

She exhaled, her cheeks flushed with color, her eyes overly bright. "Why?" she choked.

"Because this is my city and my home, and you are the outsider here. If there is to be a story, it's going to be *my* story, not yours."

"And what is that story, Signor Marcello?"

"Let's make this easier. It's always best to keep the story simple. I am Giovanni—close friends and family call me Gio, and you may call me Gio—and I shall call you Rachel."

"I prefer the formal."

"But it rings false," he answered, reaching out to lift a dark glossy tendril of hair from her cheek and carefully smooth it back from her face. Her skin was soft and so very warm and he was reminded of the kiss, and the heat and the sweetness of her mouth. Such a mouth. The things he could do to her mouth. He still felt carnal and hungry. Desire still ran hot in his veins. It was a novelty after so many months of grief and emptiness. "We are no longer strangers. We have a history. A story. And the media, I think, will be enamored with our story."

"The only story is the truth. You have a nephew you refuse to acknowledge, never mind support."

"But is he my nephew?"

"Yes, you know he is. I've sent you the birth certificate and we can do a DNA test while I'm here—"

"Proving what?" he retorted. Before she could answer, he reached for her again, his hand coiling in her long dark hair, tilting her head back to take her mouth in a long, searing kiss.

She didn't stiffen or resist. If anything, she leaned into him and he wrapped an arm around her slender frame holding her against him as he deepened the kiss, his tongue sweeping her mouth, tasting her, weakening her defenses. By the time he lifted his head, she was silent, no fight left in her. Her wide brown eyes looked up into his.

"You should never underestimate your opponent, Rachel," he said quietly, running his thumb lightly across her soft flushed cheek. "And you most definitely shouldn't have underestimated me."

CHAPTER TWO

RACHEL COULDN'T THINK. Her brain was foggy, and her body had gone to mush. She could barely control her limbs much less her wild emotions. What had just happened? And how had she lost power so quickly?

It was the kiss. The kiss had been her undoing. It was that good. *He* was that good. And if Antonio had kissed Juliet this way, Rachel almost understood why Juliet lost her head.

"Now you're going to wrap your arm about my waist," Giovanni said, his hand settling low on her back, hand warm against the base of her spine, "and we're going to retrace our steps and we'll return to my house together."

"I'm not going to—"

He captured her face, kissing her again, deeply, teasing, stroking her lips and the inside of her mouth, setting her body on fire, destroying her resistance. She reached for his sweater, clinging to the softness, needing support, but the cashmere stretched, yielding, and she leaned against his chest, unable to stand.

"Stop fighting me, and put your arm around me," he murmured, his deep voice in her ear. "You're making this more difficult than it needs to be."

Her hand turned into a fist and she pressed it against his torso, pushing back at him, angry and off balance, not sure how he'd flipped everything around, seizing control from her. His body was so warm, heat emanated from him, making her want to step closer, not farther away. It was so confusing. She pressed her fist into him, pressing against the lean, hard muscle of his torso. "You're the one playing a game, Giovanni."

"Oh, yes, and it is *my* game."

She licked the swollen fullness of her upper lip. Her mouth still tingled and throbbed from the kisses. "The rules don't make sense."

"That's because you're not thinking clearly. Later it will be clear to you."

"But that could be too late."

He stroked her hot cheek. "Very true."

That light caress made her pulse jump. Her legs still weren't steady. "You need to stop touching me."

His head dipped, his lips against her brow, and then another light kiss high on her cheekbone, his deep voice humming through her. "You shouldn't have started this."

She closed her eyes as his lips brushed her earlobe, the touch warm and light, making her skin tingle. "Stop. This is about Michael, and only Michael," she protested, but her voice was weak and she didn't sound convincing, not even to herself.

He knew, too. She could tell by the glint in his eyes, a bright fierce flash of triumph. He thought he'd won, and maybe he had won this one battle, but it was an isolated battle and he hadn't won the war. At the same time, she couldn't secure Michael's future by remaining outside, bickering.

Or kissing. Because she didn't kiss strangers. She wasn't free with her affections. If anything, she was a little nervous around men, not having a lot of confidence in herself as a woman. It'd been years since she'd been out on a proper date, and Juliet used to say that men would like her better if she'd just relax and not take herself so seriously.

It wasn't that Rachel took herself so seriously, but she didn't know how to flirt, and she wasn't about to resort to flattery just to make a man feel good. Fortunately, in her job she didn't have to flatter and charm, she just needed to know her aircraft, and she did. It was easy to be enthusiastic about luxury planes and all the different ways one could customize an AeroDynamics jet interior.

"Ready to go in?" Giovanni asked, placing a kiss on the top of her head. "Or do we need to give our photographer friends another passionate embrace?"

"No!" Reluctantly she slid her arm around his waist, shuddering as he drew her close to his hip,

and then they were walking, but she couldn't even feel her legs.

This was crazy. She couldn't wrap her head around everything that had just happened. Perhaps *he* was crazy. Perhaps she'd just thrown herself from the fire into the frying pan. Was that the expression? In her dazed state, she couldn't be sure of anything right now. His kisses... They'd wrecked her. His touch absolutely baffled her.

No one touched her. No one wanted to kiss her. And she knew he didn't really want to kiss her, but he'd done it to shift the power, seize control. It had been a shocking move but surprisingly effective. That's the part she didn't understand. When had kissing someone become the way to handle a situation? And why had it worked so well on her? She should have been able to resist him. She should have been outraged and offended and not melted.

And she had melted. Into a puddle of boneless, spineless sensation.

But now she needed to gather herself and focus and think. *Think.* She needed a new plan, and quickly.

They were crossing the pavement, approaching the palazzo, and while she dreaded entering Giovanni's home, she'd at least have Michael back.

Rachel suddenly stumbled, tripping over her own feet. His arm tightened around her, and he drew her firmly against his side. "Too close," she protested.

"I can feel you trembling. If I let you go, you'll fall."

"Blame yourself. You had no business kissing me."

"Has it been that long since you've been properly kissed?"

"I wouldn't call it a *proper* kiss. In America we don't manhandle women."

"Yes, I've heard that American men don't know how to handle women. Such a shame." They paused several feet from the door. He tilted her face up, stared into her eyes. "You look better now that you've been kissed, though. Less pale and pinched." He smiled into her eyes but there was a predatory gleam in the blue depths. "Do you want to thank me now, or later?"

She knew what he was doing, striking a pose, giving the photographers more pictures with different angles for a wide variety of shots, but it infuriated her that he'd taken her big moment and turned it into his. "This is going to end badly," she said tightly.

The corner of his mouth lifted, and he stared down into her face for a long, tense moment, before laughing shortly. "Are you just now figuring that out?"

The front door suddenly swung open, and he kept her close as they entered the palazzo, passing through the high wooden doors and into the cavernous central hall lit by an enormous Murano chandelier, at least seven feet tall, a masterpiece of sparkling glass leaves, flowers and fruits all set amongst intricate, delicate glass rods and fanciful, fragile arabesques.

A member of his staff had obviously been at the front door watching and waiting for them, as the front door opened before Giovanni could touch it, and then closed quietly behind them. Rachel turned her head, craning to see if it was the old man who'd answered the door earlier, but Giovanni was urging her forward, moving her toward the stairs.

Think, she told herself. She needed to clear her head and follow a thought all the way through instead of this—this capitulation of reason and control.

"You can let me go now," she said, shrugging to free herself. "There are no cameras here."

His arm fell away but his fingers remained low on her spine, creating insistent pressure as he marched her up the sweeping marble stairs to a formal salon on the second floor. The doors again magically closed behind them and only then did Giovanni's hand leave her.

She felt more than a little lost as she glanced around a room that could only be described as magnificent. More glittering chandeliers lined the ceiling, with matching sconces on the wall. Tall windows overlooked the canal while massive framed mirrors covered portions of the walls, the antique mirrors reflecting the gray light outside, highlighting the frescoed and plasterwork ceiling.

Rachel was out of her element but she'd never let him know. It was bad enough that he thought she'd enjoyed his kiss.

"Who has Michael?" she asked, standing stiffly in the center of the room. "Can you send for him?"

"No." Giovanni gestured for her to sit. "We have quite a lot to discuss before he joins us."

"We can talk once he's back with me."

"You left him here. I'm not about to just hand him over as if he were a lost wallet or umbrella."

"You know why I did that."

"I know you're an impulsive woman—"

"You could *not* be more wrong. I am a very calm person—" She went quiet as she saw the lift on his eyebrow. "You're making me upset. You've been impossible from the start."

"We've only just met, and it was not an auspicious first meeting, with you abandoning an infant on my doorstep, and then running from the scene."

Rachel clamped her jaw tight to keep from speaking too quickly, aware that every word could and would be used against her. She fought to control the pitch and tone of her voice. "I did not abandon him. I would not *ever* abandon him. I love him."

"Odd way of showing it, don't you think?"

"I was trying to get your attention."

"And now you have it." He gestured again toward the silk upholstered chair and sofa. "May I help you with your coat?"

"No, thank you. I won't be staying long."

He gave her an odd look, his lips twisting as if amused. "Are you sure you won't be more comfortable?"

"I'll be more comfortable when I have the baby."

"He's in good hands at the moment, and we have a great deal to discuss before he joins us. So I do suggest you try to be comfortable, since the conversation probably won't be." Gio's gaze rested intently on her face before dropping to study the rest of her. "It's been an unusually eventful morning. I'm sending for a coffee. Would you like one?"

She shook her head, and then changed her mind. "Yes, please."

He reached for his phone from a pocket and shot off a message. "Coffee should be here soon," he said, sitting down in the pale blue silk armchair facing the upholstered sofa. He stretched his legs before him, looking at ease. "Are you quite certain you wish to stand for the rest of the day?"

His tone was lazy, almost indulgent, and it provoked her more than if he'd spoken to her sternly. She felt her face flush and her body warm. "I certainly have no intention of being here more than a half hour at most."

"You think we can sort out Michael's future in thirty minutes or less?"

He sounded pleasant and reasonable, too reasonable, and it put her on guard, hands clenching at her sides, knuckles aching with the tightness of the grip. He was easier to fight when he was defensive and angry. Now she felt as if she were the difficult one.

It wasn't fair but clearly he didn't play by any rules but his own.

Drawing a quick breath, she sat down on the edge of the small wood framed sofa, the elegant and delicate shape popular hundreds of years ago, the silver silk fabric gleaming with bits of red and pale blue threads.

She folded her hands in her lap, waiting for him to speak. It was a tactic that worked well with her wealthy clients. They preferred being in control, and they felt most in control when they could dictate the conversation. She'd let Gio direct the conversation. He'd think he was in charge that way and she could use the time to regroup and plan.

But Giovanni was in no hurry to speak. He leaned back in his chair, legs extended, and watched her.

There was no sound in the grand room. No ticking clock. No creaking of any sort. Just silence, and the silence was excruciating.

Her pulse quickened as time stretched, lengthening, testing her patience. Her nerves felt wound to a breaking point. She exhaled hard. "If we don't speak it will definitely take longer than a half hour to sort out Michael's future," she said shortly, irritated beyond reason with Giovanni. He was playing a game with her even now, and it made her impossibly angry.

"I was giving you time to compose yourself," he answered with a faint smile. "You were trembling so much earlier I thought you could use a bit of time for rest and reflection."

"It was cold and damp and windy outside. I was freezing, thus the shivers. It's a natural reaction when chilled."

"Are you cold now?"

"No, this room is heated. It's quite nice in here."

One of his black brows lifted ever so slightly but he didn't speak, and her stomach did a nervous flip-flop.

He was toying with her deliberately. She was certain he wanted to make her uneasy. But why? Did he think she'd collapse into tears? She didn't like the silence but it was preferable to being held and touched. She had an excellent head for business and had proven herself remarkably good at establishing and maintaining professional relationships, but personal relationships, those were problematic.

She hadn't dated enough when she was younger. Although it'd be tempting to blame the opposite sex for failing to notice her, it wasn't entirely true.

She lacked confidence and had failed to put herself out there. Dating seemed to require too much energy and effort, with too many ups and downs to make the dashed dreams and rejection worthwhile.

Instead she focused on work, pouring herself into the job, earning promotions and bonuses as well as praise from senior management. While other young women her age were busy falling in love and needing time off for romantic weekends and holidays, she closed deals and made AeroDynamics money and found tremendous satisfaction in being the one everyone could count on for being there and doing what needed to be done.

Which was all very good and well at the corporate office, but sitting here in this enormous room, facing a tall, handsome, charismatic Italian, she was secretly terrified. She could sell a man a thirty-million-dollar airplane, but she fell apart when kissed, especially if the kiss was dark and sexual, destroying all rational thought.

"The silence is soothing, is it not?" she asked, struggling to sound as relaxed as he appeared.

He seemed to check a smile, grooves bracketing his firm mouth. "Indeed."

"I hope we can drink our coffee in silence. Silence makes everything better," she added, frustration growing. "Especially when it's in such an impressive room." She glanced around the salon, the proportions alone overwhelming, never mind the grand paintings and light fixtures. "I suppose you hoped to intimidate me by bringing me here to your grand salon."

"This is not by any means my most impressive room. It's actually one of the smaller salons on this floor, considered by most to be intimate and welcoming." His lashes dropped, concealing the intense blue of his eyes. "It's my mother's favorite. If she were here, she'd serve you coffee here."

Embarrassed, Rachel bit her lip and glanced away, more self-conscious and resentful than ever. Two weeks ago, when her private investigator gave her Giovanni's address and she realized she'd have to come to Venice to get him to meet with her, she'd pictured meeting him somewhere neutral and public, perhaps at her hotel in one of the cheerful pleasant rooms downstairs, or maybe a quiet restaurant tucked away off the more public thoroughfares.

She'd imagined he'd be proud and arrogant, possibly grim and unsmiling. It hadn't once crossed her mind that he'd kiss her, and then walk her into his home and shut the door and create this awful air of privacy. Intimacy. She swallowed hard and struggled to think of something to say. "Does your mother live here?"

"Part of the year. During the winter she likes to go to her sister's in Sorrento." He rose from his chair and walked toward the wall of tall windows, pausing before one window, his gaze fixed intently on a distant point.

She wondered if he was looking for the photographers, or if there was something else happening on the lagoon. She used the opportunity to study him. He was easily six-two, maybe taller, and his shoulders were broad, his spine long, tapering to a lean waist and powerful legs. Even from the back he crackled with authority and power. He was not the recluse she'd imagined.

Still staring out, Gio added, "I confess, I'm surprised you never reached out to her. I would have thought that in your desperation you would have approached her. Who to better love and accept a bambino than the grandmother?"

She folded her hands in her lap. "I did reach out."

He turned to look at her. "And?"

"She wasn't interested."

"Is that what she said?"

"No. She never responded."

"She probably didn't get your messages then."

"I didn't just call. I wrote letters, too."

"All sent to the Marcello corporate office in Rome?"

Rachel nodded.

His shoulders shifted. "Then that is why she didn't receive them. Anything to my mother would go to my assistant, and my assistant wouldn't forward."

"Why not? It was important correspondence."

"My assistant was under strict instructions to not disturb my mother with anything troubling, or upsetting. My mother hasn't been well for a while."

"I would imagine that she'd be delighted to discover that Antonio had left a piece of him behind."

"I can't—and won't—get her hopes up, not if she is being used, or manipulated."

"I wouldn't do that to her."

"No? You wouldn't have asked her for money if she'd responded? You wouldn't have demanded support?" He saw her expression and smiled grimly. "You would have, and you know it. I do, too, which is why I had to protect her, and shield her from stress."

"I would think that having a beautiful grandson—Antonio's son—in her arms would help her heal."

"If the child in question really was Antonio's... maybe."

"Michael *is* Antonio's."

"I don't know that."

"I have proof."

"DNA tests?" he mocked, walking again, now prowling the perimeter of the room. "I'll do my own, thank you."

"*Good.* Do them. I've been waiting for you to do your own!"

He paused, arms crossing over his chest. "And if he is Antonio's, what then?"

"You accept him," she said.

His dark head tipped as he considered her. "Accept him. What does that even mean?"

She opened her mouth to answer, and then closed it without making a sound. Her heart did an uneven thump and suddenly it hurt to breathe. Michael needed support—not just financial, but emotional. She wanted to be sure Michael wasn't forgotten, not by her family, or Antonio's.

It was bad enough that Michael had been left an orphan within months of his birth, but the way Juliet died… It was wrong, and it continued to eat at Rachel because she hadn't understood how badly Juliet was doing. She'd been oblivious to the depth of Juliet's despair. Rachel could now write an entire pamphlet on postpartum depression, but back in November and December she hadn't understood it, and she hadn't been properly sympathetic. Instead of getting Juliet medical help, she'd given her sister tough love, and it was absolutely the wrong thing to do.

It had only made everything so much worse. It was without exaggeration, the beginning of the end. And it was all Rachel's fault.

Rachel had failed Juliet when her sister needed her most.

CHAPTER THREE

GIOVANNI WATCHED RACHEL'S eyes fill with tears and her lips part, then seal shut, her teeth biting down into the soft lower lip as though she was fighting to stay in control.

He didn't buy the act, as it was an act.

Adelisa had been the same. Beautiful, bright and spirited, she'd captured his heart from the start. He'd proposed before the end of the first year, and delighted in buying her the pretty—but expensive—trinkets her heart desired.

Her heart desired many.

Diamonds and rubies, emeralds and sapphires—jewels she ended up liquidating almost as quickly as he gave them to her. Not that he knew what happened to them until much later.

His family warned him that Adelisa was using him. His mother came to him privately on three different occasions, sharing her fears, and then reporting on rumors that Adelisa had been seen with other men, but he didn't believe it. He was sure Adelisa loved him. She wore his engagement ring.

She was eagerly planning their wedding. Why would she betray him?

Six months later he heard about a pair of stunning diamond earrings for sale, a pair rumored to come from the Marcello family. He tracked down the earrings and the jeweler, and they were a pair of a set he'd given Adelisa the night of their engagement party. They were worth millions of dollars, but more than that, they were family heirlooms and something he gave with his heart.

He was stunned, and worse, humiliated. His mother had been right. He'd been duped. And everyone seemed to have known the truth but him.

It'd been ten years since that humiliation, but Gio still avoided love and emotional entanglements. Far better to enjoy a purely physical relationship than be played for a fool. And now his narrowed gaze swept over Rachel, from the classic oval shape of her pretty face to the glossy length of her ponytail with the windswept tendrils. She was neither tall nor petite, but average height and an average build, although in her dark coat, which hit just above her black knee-high leather boots, she looked polished and pretty.

He didn't want her to be pretty, though. He didn't want to find anything about her attractive or desirable, and yet he was aware of her, just as he was aware that beneath her winter coat, there were curves, generous curves, because he'd felt them when he'd drawn her against him, her body

pressed to his. "So what is your plan?" he asked
tautly. "Have you sorted out how you intend to get
us to accept the child? Because a family is not just
DNA. A family is nurture, and relationships, and
those develop over years. You can't simply force
one to accept an outsider—"

"Michael is not an outsider. He's Antonio's
son." She'd gone pale, her expression strained.
"And my sister's son," she added after a half beat,
"and I know you have no love for my sister, but
she cared for your brother, deeply—"

"We're in private now. You can drop the script.
There's no need for theatrics."

"You don't even know the facts."

"I know enough."

"Well, I thought I did, too, but I was wrong, and
Juliet's no longer here because I got it wrong. Michael has no one but us and you can think what
you want of Juliet, and me, but I insist you give
him a chance—" She broke off as the door opened
and a young, slim, dark-haired woman entered
carrying a huge, ornate silver tray filled with silver pots and smaller sterling silver dishes along
with a pair of china cups and saucers.

Rachel was grateful for the interruption. She
needed a moment to compose herself. She still
felt so rattled by his kisses. There had been nothing light or friendly in the way he took her mouth,
claiming her as if she belonged to him, shaping
her to his frame. She did not belong to him, and

to have his tongue stroke the inside of her mouth, creating the dark seductive rhythm that made her body ache—

The sound of Giovanni speaking to the maid broke her train of thought. Heart thudding, Rachel knotted her hands in her lap, realizing she hadn't just gotten Giovanni's attention, she'd given him control. She'd wanted his assistance, but clearly help would be on his terms, not hers.

The young maid placed the silver tray on a table next to the couch, not far from where Rachel was sitting, before leaving.

Giovanni crossed to take one espresso and handed her the other.

Rachel took the small cup and saucer. "When will you permit Michael to join us?"

"As soon as he's finished his bottle."

"He's awake then?"

"Yes."

"And he's okay?"

"Apparently my staff is already besotted with him. Anna said the girls are fighting over who is to hold him next."

"Allow me to resolve the argument. Send for him, and I'll hold him."

"You haven't had your coffee yet."

"I can multitask."

"And deprive my staff of the opportunity to kiss and cuddle a baby?"

"But by keeping him from me, you deprive me."

"Is it such a deprivation?" Gio's voice was pitched low. "I would think it's a relief. Your letters made it sound as if you were at your wit's end—exhausted, and overwhelmed, close to breaking."

She flushed. "You read my letters."

"As did my attorneys."

Heat rushed down her neck, flooding her limbs. "So you were stonewalling me."

"I had my own investigation to do."

"You took your time."

"I don't respond well to threats."

"I never threatened you!"

"Your letters demanded I act before I was prepared to—"

"This isn't about you! It's about a child who has lost both his parents. It's selfish to deny him a chance at a better life."

"We've returned to the material demands, haven't we?"

"Material is only part of it. There is the cultural aspect, as well. The baby might have been born in Seattle but he is only half-American, and he needs to know you, his father's family. He needs to be part of you."

"Why aren't you enough?"

"I'm not Italian, or Venetian."

"And you think that's important?"

"Yes."

His lips compressed, his jaw firming "I doubt you value his Venetian ancestry and heritage as much as you value the Marcellos' wealth and clout."

"Can't I want both for him?"

"But I don't think you really want both."

"That's not true. I've worked hard to get to where I am now, but even with an excellent job, I barely make ends meet. And as a single woman, not yet twenty-nine, I'm in no position to raise a child on my own, much less a Marcello—"

"What does that even mean to you? A Marcello?"

"Your family is old, and respected. Your history goes back hundreds of years. The Marcellos have contributed significantly to modern Italy, but you personally have done so much for Italy's economy that just last year you were awarded the Order of Merit for Labor." She saw his black eyebrow arch, his expression almost mocking. "And yes," she added defiantly. "I did my homework. I had to in order to find you."

"Fourteen years ago the Marcello holding company was on the verge of bankruptcy. No one wanted to do business with us. No one trusted us. I have poured myself into the company to rebuild it, sacrificing a personal life in order to make the business my focus. And so, yes, I know manufacturing, construction and real estate, but I'm not interested in expanding the family."

"But the family has been expanded," she said quietly. "With or without your consent."

"You're revealing your hand," he replied. "I see where you're going with this. How we all owe him, because he is my brother's son. His heir."

"That's not where I'm going."

"No? You're not about to play the Marcello heir card?"

She dampened her lips, trying to hide her sudden flurry of nerves because she had played that card, and she'd played it with the press. "I'm not asking for a piece of your company. I'm not wanting Michael to inherit Marcello shares or stock, but I do believe you can, and should, give Michael a proper education and the advantages I could not provide for him."

Giovanni's lip curled. "You didn't ever want to leave Michael here. In fact, you never intended to actually let him go. How could you? You wouldn't be able to justify the child support you feel you deserve."

"This isn't about me."

"Isn't it? Because let's be honest, a six-month-old has very few material needs. Milk, a dry diaper, clean clothes—"

"Time, love, attention."

"Which you want to be compensated for."

"*No*," she said sharply, before holding her breath and counting to ten. She had to stay calm. She couldn't get into a fight, not now, not before anything was settled, and certainly not before Michael had been returned to her. "I wish I didn't need your money. I'd love it if I didn't need help. I'd love to be able to tell you to go fly a kite—" She hesitated as she saw him arch a brow. "It's an expression."

"I'm familiar with it."

"I was trying to be polite."

"Of course."

His sarcasm made her want to take a poker iron from the fireplace and beat him with it, which was something, considering the fact that she was not a violent person, and did not go through life wanting to hit things, much less human beings. "I don't want to be compensated. But I can't work and care for Michael at the same time, nor does AeroDynamics provide an on-site nursery. The fact is, there is no solution for child care for someone in my position."

"That problem disappears, though, if you claim Antonio's assets in the Marcello holding company, allowing you to retire from your job and raise the child in the comfort and style he deserves." Giovanni's blue gaze held hers, his mocking tone matching his cynical expression. "Have I got it right?"

Offended, she stiffened. "You've created a fascinating story, but it's not true."

"Do you share the same father and mother as your sister?"

"Yes."

"So you were raised in the same…struggling… blue-collar household?"

She heard the way he emphasized *struggling* and winced. "We were not a blue-collar household. My father was a respected engineer for Boeing. He was brilliant. And my mother managed the front office of a successful Seattle dental practice."

"Not Seattle, but Burien."

So he had done some research, and he'd found her family wanting.

She battled her temper, not wanting to lose control again. It was one thing to become muddled by a kiss, but another to allow his words to stir her up. "Yes, Burien, just a few miles south of downtown Seattle. Living in a suburb was a lifestyle choice. That way my mother could work and be available to see us to the school bus before school, and then meet our bus afterward. She juggled a lot, especially after our father died."

"Money was an issue."

Her smile was gracious. She would be gracious and serene. "Being middle class is not a crime, nor does it reflect badly on my family. Wealth doesn't make one superior."

"It does give one advantages...physically, socially, psychologically."

"But not morally." She held her smile, hiding her fury. She'd met many arrogant, condescending men at AeroDynamics but they'd never shamed her for having less. "Morally you are not superior in any way. In fact, I'd say morally you are inferior because you've refused so far to do what is right. You're more concerned about protecting your corporation than your nephew—"

"We were discussing wealth and its advantages, and you've turned it into an attack."

"Not *attacking*, just stating my position."

"That you are morally superior because you're of the working class?"

"If I'm morally superior it's because I didn't turn my back on my nephew like you!" She drew a shallow breath, stomach churning. "I knew your brother. He was my client and he'd be devastated that you've rejected his son—"

"I haven't rejected my nephew, and you could not have known my brother well if you thought he was pleased in any way about your sister's pregnancy. Her pregnancy devastated him. It hastened his death, so before you lecture me about moral superiority, why don't you look at your own family?"

Her lips opened and closed but she couldn't make a sound.

Giovanni rose. "Your sister is a classic gold digger. She wanted a rich man and she found one in Antonio. She didn't care that he was ill and dying. She didn't care that she was making excessive demands. All she wanted was her way, and she got it. So save your speeches, Rachel. I know just who you and your sister are. Master manipulators, but I won't be played. Good day. *Addio*."

He walked out, leaving the door open behind him.

* * *

Giovanni climbed the staircase two steps at a time, anger rolling through him, anger and outrage that a stranger would try to tell him who his brother was and what his brother wanted.

Growing up, Antonio had been Giovanni's best friend. They'd had a younger sister but she'd died at six, which had only brought Antonio and Gio closer together. Antonio and Gio were so close that Gio, an introvert, didn't feel the need to have a lot of other friends.

They ended up attending the same boarding school in England, and then the same university. Antonio loved business and finance while Giovanni preferred engineering and construction, which made them a good pair, and they both looked forward to working together at the Marcello corporate office, which is what Gio did right after graduating from university. But Antonio went on to graduate school, earning an MBA from Harvard. Giovanni had been the one to convince their father that it was a smart investment, sending Antonio to America for the prestigious program, as he'd be able to bring his knowledge back to Marcello corporate office afterward.

It didn't work out that way, though. While at Harvard, Antonio was introduced to a big financial firm on Wall Street and they were impressed with his mind and his linguistic ability—Antonio, like Giovanni, spoke five languages fluently. The firm courted him, wanting him to work for them in their Manhattan office. Antonio accepted the offer as it was extremely lucrative and involved a great deal of travel and perks that he wouldn't get working for the family business.

Giovanni was shocked by his younger brother's decision. It'd felt like a betrayal. Marcello Enterprises was in trouble. Their father had made years of bad decisions, and Giovanni, the practical, pragmatic engineer, needed his brother to help save the company. Without Antonio they could lose everything. But Antonio wasn't eager to work for a company that was floundering—even if it was his family's.

Gio met Adelisa right after Antonio accepted the position in Manhattan, and he'd shared with her his disappointment, and his frustration. She'd been a good listener. Too good a listener, actually, as she would later share company secrets with others, undermining everything Gio had worked so hard to accomplish.

Of course, not all women were like Adelisa. But when you were one of the wealthiest men in Italy, it was hard to trust any woman's motives.

Toronto Public Library
Don Mills
888 Lawrence Ave E
416-395-5710

- Checkout Receipt -
Sep 23, 2019 3:18 PM

**Library
Card:** ***********5733

Number of items: 5

Item ID: 37131208131078
Title: ADULT FICTION
Date Due: Oct 15, 2019

Item ID: 3713118531
Title: ADULT FIC 20
Date Due: Oc 842
9120
Item ID: T F2019
Title: O
208056753
Item I FICTION
Titl Oct 15, 201
ID: 37131208
e: ADULT FI
Date Due: OC

Tele

CHAPTER FOUR

FOR A LONG moment after Giovanni walked out, Rachel sat frozen on the couch, thoughts blank, heart on fire, Gio's sharp words ringing in her head preventing her from thinking or feeling anything other than pain and shame.

Gio was right, and wrong. But more right than wrong. Juliet *had* wanted a wealthy boyfriend. She'd wanted to marry a very rich man and it had been her goal since she was in junior high school.

Juliet felt she deserved better than everyone else. She wasn't ordinary like Rachel. She was beautiful. She'd been a pretty baby and had grown into a little girl who turned heads. Juliet knew it, too, and from the time she was small she dazzled everyone she met.

It started with their parents, and then Juliet turned her charm onto her teachers, and she went through life wrapping everyone around her little finger.

It seemed to Rachel that she was the only one Juliet couldn't manipulate, and over the years it created tension between them and friction in the family. Juliet would have a tantrum when Rachel refused to capitulate to her demands, and then Mother would intercede, and inevitably she took Juliet's side. Mother had been firmly on Juliet's side last spring when Juliet began dating Antonio and needed loans to buy new clothes and pay for expensive hair and skin appointments.

Rachel had refused to give her sister money for a new wardrobe, telling Juliet to do what everyone else did and look for employment so she could buy new clothes with money she'd earned. "She'd have more self-respect," Rachel told their mother when Juliet had the expected meltdown. "It's not right to give Juliet everything she wants."

"Why are you so hard on her?" Mother answered. "She's not cut out for business the way you are."

"That's not true. She's smart, Mom. She's just really lazy."

"You're so grumpy all the time, Rachel. Where's your sense of humor?"

"I *have* a sense of humor, but it's hard to feel like laughing when Juliet can't hold down a job. She lives off loans from you and me."

"It's been months since we've floated her any money. She's getting better at managing her funds."

"Because her bills are getting paid for by one boyfriend or another."

"At least she has a boyfriend."

"Wanting a boyfriend isn't exactly aspirational!"

"Oh, yes, that's right, Rach. You're far too intelligent to fall in love."

"No, Mom. I'm not too intelligent to fall in love. But I'm too intelligent to turn a man into a meal ticket." She paused but her mother was silent now and Rachel pressed on. "I should think you'd be uncomfortable with Juliet always trying to cash in from her looks. She doesn't think she should have to work because she's beautiful but good looks can only take one so far—"

"You're jealous."

"Mom, I'm too old for this. I might have been jealous when I was fourteen and she was twelve and Juliet stole my first boyfriend, but I'm twenty-eight and I have great friends, a job I love and a life I enjoy."

"Then why care that Juliet is doing life her way? Don't resent her happiness. She's sure she's found the one, and I fully expect an engagement announcement any day now."

But Mrs. Bern was wrong. There was no engagement, but there was an announcement. Juliet was pregnant and her rich boyfriend, Italian businessman, Antonio Marcello, had broken things off with Juliet and returned to Italy without her.

It had been a terrible time in Seattle afterward. Juliet had been heartbroken, and then not even two months later, Mother died. They hadn't known she was unwell. Mother hadn't even known. If there was a blessing, it was that Mother went quickly, without months of suffering. She was there one day and then gone the next.

Not even three weeks later, they learned through a newspaper article that Antonio Marcello had died in Rome, at home, with his family at his side.

Juliet never really recovered after that. First Mother, then Antonio, and Juliet still had the third trimester to get through, but there had been too many hits and shocks. She went into labor depressed and didn't bounce back after delivery.

Rachel had been impatient with Juliet in the months following Michael's birth. She'd tried to hide her irritation, and she'd given her pep talks, perhaps more vigorous than necessary, but Rachel was overwhelmed by Juliet's depression and her sister's inability to care for the baby. Work was stressful with rounds of layoffs due to the economic downturn, and God knows, they needed Rachel to be employed. She was the only one keeping the family afloat.

But Rachel was barely coping herself. Mom was gone, Juliet wouldn't get out of bed, the baby needed looking after and Rachel didn't know what had happened to her life.

It wasn't her life anymore.

A light knock sounded on the open door. Rachel looked up to see the young maid, Anna, standing in the doorway.

"Please, follow me," Anna said in stilted English.

"Where?" Rachel asked, unable to move.

"I am to...walk you...to the door."

"Where is my baby?"

Anna frowned.

"Michael. The bambino," Rachel said, setting the cup down. "I cannot leave without him."

"Sorry. Signor, he said the bambino he stays here. You...go." She gestured to the door. "You come with me, please?"

"No. Absolutely not. I'm not leaving Michael here. Bring me the baby. *Now*."

"I am sorry. I cannot. Signor will telephone you later, yes?"

Rachel was on her feet, crossing the room. "Where is he? Where is Signor Marcello?"

"He has gone to his office. I will show you to... down the stairs. Please come—" Anna broke off as Rachel brushed past her, stepping into the hall.

"Where is his office? Which direction?" Rachel demanded.

"No. Sorry."

Rachel's gaze swept the hall, certain that there were only more formal rooms on this floor. She glanced right, to the marble stairs they'd climbed earlier. The wide gleaming steps continued up at least another two floors.

She headed for the stairs and quickly climbed up. Anna chased after her, speaking in a stream of broken English and Italian.

Rachel ignored the girl. "Giovanni," she called, her voice echoing in the stairwell. "Gio! Where are you?"

Her voice bounced off the marble and the high ceiling, but she wouldn't stop until she found him. "I'm not leaving here, not without Michael. So if you want me to go, Gio, give me Michael and I'll go, but there is no way I'd leave—"

"Enough." A door at the end of the hall opened abruptly, and Giovanni appeared, expression dark. "You've done nothing but create a circus since you arrived this morning. My staff is not accustomed to screaming and shouting."

"They are Italian. I seriously doubt they are shocked by genuine emotion," she retorted, marching down the hall toward him. "And you... How could you just go and leave me there like that?"

"I said goodbye. You were the one who refused to leave."

"You knew I wouldn't go without Michael."

"You didn't seem to have a problem leaving him here earlier." He stared down at her, blue eyes snapping fire. "Are you sure you and your sister are not twins?"

He couldn't have said anything more hurtful if he'd tried. Her eyes smarted and her throat sealed closed.

Giovanni was arrogant and condescending and lacked even the smallest shred of human compassion. Thank God he didn't intimidate her. She'd worked with dozens of powerful men over the past five years, men who had incredible power and staggering fortunes and egos to match. They all liked to be flattered. They all felt entitled. They all needed to be right. Giovanni was no different. She'd never get what she wanted if she fought him. If she angered him. If she continued to alienate him.

Alienating him would just hurt Michael, and that wouldn't be fair or right. Juliet had made mistakes. Her life had become such a mess. But Michael wasn't a mess. Michael was pure and innocent, and that innocence had to be protected. Yes, she'd failed Juliet, but there was no way she'd fail Michael.

And so, even though a dozen different things came to mind, protests and rebukes, in the end her feelings didn't matter. *She* didn't matter. This was about her nephew, who'd been left without a mother or a father and needed someone to champion him. And that someone was her.

"I don't care what you think of me," she said unsteadily, "but I do care what you think about Michael. He did not ask to be born. He is innocent in all this. And whether you like it or not, he carries your brother's name, and DNA, and if I have to go to your court to get him proper child support, I will."

"I don't doubt you would, but you'd find that our courts move at a snail's pace compared to your courts. You could be waiting for six or eight, or even ten years, for any type of legal decision."

That knocked her back, thoughts scattering, but then she managed a careless shrug and found her voice. "You're happy to wage a public war for that long? It seems so unlike you, considering how much you value your privacy."

He shot her a look she couldn't quite decipher. "So let's put our cards on the table. Let's stop with the games. How much are you asking for him?"

"How much child support?" she asked, needing to clarify his question.

"No. How much do you want for him? How much will it cost to take him off your hands permanently?"

CHAPTER FIVE

For a second Rachel couldn't breathe. The air bottled in her lungs until they ached, and her head felt light and dizzy. She exhaled on a gasp. "You…*want*…him?"

"That is probably stretching the truth."

"Then why are you even asking?"

"Maybe I'm curious as to what it would take to get you out of my life."

"So you don't really want him—you just want to be rid of me."

"I want the problem to disappear, yes."

"But the problem would be living in your palazzo. Unless you sent him elsewhere. Boarding school for infants, maybe?"

He gave her a long, hard look. "He would not be mistreated."

"Would he be loved?"

"My family is not in the habit of abusing children."

"That's not the same thing as being cherished and adored—"

"He would be raised the way Antonio and I

were raised. With equal parts love and discipline."

"And would you be the one to raise him?"

"That's something to still be sorted out."

"I couldn't give you an answer then, not without knowing who'd raise him. Financial support is important but his care...the affection he receives...is everything and will determine not just his health but his happiness."

"I wasn't raised in the Dark Ages. I know children need affection."

"Would you be able to give him a mother, or would you hire a nanny?"

"I am not about to find a wife just to give him a mother. I'd hire a nanny."

"Would you be able to spend significant time with him?"

"I am a bachelor. I work long hours. But I would ensure that my nephew had the best care money could buy."

That sounded awful. She suppressed a shiver.

One of his black brows lifted. "What's wrong? You don't look happy."

"He deserves more than an expensive nanny."

"She'd be well-trained and dedicated—"

"I think I've heard enough. You've painted a dreadful picture. There is no way I could leave Michael to your care."

"But you were so insistent that Michael be raised as a Marcello!"

"Is that how you were raised? With the best nanny money could buy?"

"Yes, and the best boarding schools, before attending the best universities."

"You didn't grow up here at home?"

"No. And I turned out well, wouldn't you say?"

"You turned out heartless."

"I'm practical, not heartless. There is a difference."

"Well, I want him loved, and protected, so no, you can't buy me off. I'm not going to abandon him."

"But isn't that what you did earlier? You handed him to my steward and walked away without a backward glance."

"It was a desperate ploy to get your attention, and it worked."

"Desperate people have a price. I know you have yours."

"I'm not that desperate."

"Then go back to Seattle, Rachel, and stop wasting my time." He turned around and walked away from her, entering the room with the open door.

The sharpness in his voice made her chest tighten and her stomach fall. Was he really so cold and callous or was he testing her? Either way, she was here, and she was not about to be scared off.

She followed him into the room. "Life is not

black or white, Gio, and I don't believe in all or nothing. I believe in discussion and compromise— even when it's uncomfortable. We need to find a middle ground—" She stopped as she noticed the soaring stone arches that divided the large room into two. On one side of the beige arches was a massive desk and chair, and on the other was a wall of windows framed in stained wood, topped by clear leaded glass and Palladian style arches. The high ceiling was paneled in dark wood and beams. The marble floor was the color of vanilla and matched the warm plaster walls, while the white slipcovered furniture in the sitting area looked effortlessly chic. This, she thought, was what people meant when they said Italians had style.

She worked with designers on a daily basis, creating custom plane interiors, but this took her breath away. It was visually stunning. History reimagined. Luxury reinvented. "Incredible," she murmured. She didn't know what she loved more—the soaring stone arches that looked as if they'd been lifted from ancient ruins, or the magnificent leaded glass windows that allowed the light to deeply penetrate the room.

"Your office?" she asked, still marveling over the elegant simplicity. No mirrors or gilded surfaces here. No Murano glass. No shimmering sconces. Just dark wood, stone pediments over tall doorways, marble slab floors and windows that allowed light to spill everywhere, brightening surfaces and reflecting off the white furniture.

"Yes." He'd taken a seat on the edge of his dark desk and watched her do a slow turn in the middle of the room.

"It's beautiful."

"Thank you."

She approached one of the arches and ran her hand across the surface. "How much of this is original?"

"All of it. This floor was private, built for the family, not for entertaining. I asked my designer to make a few modifications, but the building dates back to the late fifteenth century and we protected the architecture."

"What did she change?"

"The marble floor is new. The plaster has been patched and repaired. We stripped off the coat of paint that had been applied to the windows and then stained the wood to match the beams."

"I can see why you want to work here. I would want to work here."

"With technology one can work from anywhere, and I can accomplish far more here than in a noisy office with endless interruptions." He exhaled, expression shuttering. "You were saying about a middle ground?"

She hesitated. "Can we find one?" When he didn't immediately reply, she added, "I don't expect us to become friends. But if we could try to become…allies, just for our nephew's sake, I think it would help him. He doesn't have a lot of family anymore, which is why it would be nice if his surviving family could be cordial."

Giovanni didn't know how to answer her. He'd been furious when he'd walked out of the silver salon earlier, insulted that she'd lecture him on how his own brother would have felt. She had no idea how close he and his brother had been, or how much he'd grieved for Antonio this past year.

He turned away, faced the window, biting back the sharp words he wanted to say. "The baby. He is healthy?"

"Yes. Michael's meeting all his milestones, and more." She drew a breath. "Would it be possible to please send for him now? I realize that I must appear indifferent to you with regards to Michael—"

"You do not appear indifferent at all."

"But perhaps not as attached as I am. I am very attached." She drew another quick breath, her voice thickening. "I've been in his life since his birth, and I've taken care of him from the beginning when Juliet wasn't able to. And then once she was gone, it was just him and me."

He said nothing, letting her talk, because he'd been curious about this very thing. What had Michael's early months been like? Who had been part of his life?

She continued, filling the uncomfortable silence. "So you can see why I'm anxious to have him back in my arms, and why I find this all so very difficult. We've spent a great deal of time together these past few months…in fact, we've spent all our time together these past few months, and I'm missing him. Terribly, as a matter of fact."

Giovanni did not want to like her, or care about her in any way, but it was impossible to not feel anything when tears clung to her lashes and her voice was hoarse with emotion. She was either an incredible actress or she deeply cared for the child.

"Would you please send for him now?" she asked, her gaze meeting his and holding it. "Please?"

He wasn't ready to return the child to a woman who'd abandon him to a stranger, but her husky, tearful request softened his resistance. She sounded sincere, as well as anxious, and Giovanni reached into his pocket and drew out his phone to send a text message to his housekeeper, requesting that the child be brought in. "There," he said quietly, "He should be here soon."

"Thank you," she said gratefully, shooting him a smile.

Her smile knocked him off balance. It shaped her generous mouth, tilting the corners up, rounding her cheeks and warming her dark brown eyes. She was an attractive woman, but when she smiled she was positively beautiful.

He frowned, irritated with himself for noticing. He didn't want to find her beautiful. Nor did he want to remember how she'd felt outside by the canal, her slim body pressed to his, all curves and soft warmth. Just because she was soft and warm, didn't mean her heart was pure or her intentions good.

A light knock sounded on the open office door and Anna entered carrying the child, who was now awake and squirming, making fretful cries. Anna glanced at him, and he nodded at Rachel.

Rachel moved forward, meeting the maid partway, eagerly taking the infant, cuddling him close to her breast. She kissed the top of his head, and then his temple, and crooned something in his ear. The baby stopped crying. She kissed him again, gently rocking him and he lifted his head after a moment and looked up into her eyes and smiled.

A knot formed in Giovanni's chest. He glanced away, uncomfortable. Here, supposedly, was his brother's son, and yet Gio was an outsider.

It crossed his mind that maybe he had waited too long to become acquainted with his nephew. In trying to be cautious and thorough with his investigation, he'd allowed Rachel to bond with the child. If he wasn't careful, she might run and disappear with Michael. He couldn't allow that to happen. He'd lost Antonio. He couldn't lose Antonio's only child.

Giovanni stepped around to the front of his desk, and moved a pile of papers to a different corner, and then closed a file on his lap. "Michael likes you," he said casually.

Rachel froze. For a second she'd forgotten all about Gio, which seemed impossible now that she was looking up at him. Giovanni Marcello was not a man you'd ever forget. His energy was intense, and at times, overwhelming. "I love him," she answered.

"You really didn't have any intention of leaving him here, did you?"

"I prayed I wouldn't have to get into the water taxi, and I didn't."

"But what if I hadn't come out? Would you have gone?"

"I would have returned to my hotel and waited for you there." She kissed one of Michael's small fists, his skin soft and damp. The small hand had been in his mouth just moments ago. She wrinkled her nose, which made Michael laugh. "I would have waited for maybe twenty, thirty minutes, but if you hadn't come by then, I would have returned here."

"And done what?"

"Broken down your door. Screamed bloody murder."

"It didn't make you uneasy, leaving him here?"

Her heart did a painful beat as guilt assailed her. "It terrified me." She nuzzled Michael's cheek, breathing in his sweet baby scent. "But the future was equally terrifying, and so I did what I thought I had to do, believing that ultimately, you would emerge, and you would help, and you'd make sure that your brother's son would be raised by those who loved him."

Giovanni sat down in his desk chair and leaned back. "How could you have so much faith in a stranger, when you knew I'd rejected all your other attempts to see me?

"Because Antonio had such faith in you." She saw his expression darken and she felt a pang of anxiety, but she'd started down this path and had to finish. Fighting the flurry of nerves, she lightly patted the baby's back, as much to soothe him as to calm herself. "He said you were the best of the best and absolutely trustworthy. He'd said more than once that the Marcellos would not have what they do today if it wasn't for you and your sacrifices."

"It's never a sacrifice when you're helping your family."

"But you still gave up your needs for theirs."

"Just what did Antonio tell you?" he asked. "I'm interested in knowing. It would help keep his memory alive."

She shot him a look over the baby's head. It was obvious that Giovanni wasn't asking so much as commanding her to share. She smiled faintly, thinking how nice it must be to have so much power over others. He wasn't just accustomed to people doing *what* he wanted, but *when* he wanted it and exactly the *way* he wanted it.

He must have caught the curve of her lips. "You're smiling," he said.

Her shoulders twisted. "I was just thinking we're so different, and our expectations are so different. I arrived here in Venice, shaking and nervous, so nervous that I hadn't slept in days and couldn't eat. I was so worried about the outcome. I was certain you'd refuse me, certain you wouldn't see us, but hoping, praying, you might." She was talking too much, practically babbling, but she couldn't stop herself now that she'd begun. "You see, I came prepared to plead and beg, fight and cry. I came determined to get on my knees if need be—"

"You are aware that is not how you presented yourself this morning at my front door? There was no begging or pleading. You showed up armed and dangerous."

"We both know that first impressions matter. If I started out weak, you wouldn't have respected me or taken my request seriously. And I need you to respect me, not because it will change me, or the outcome of my life, but because it will change Michael's."

Giovanni looked at her from beneath his lashes, his blue gaze piercing, assessing, his firm mouth pressed into an uncompromising line. But something *had* changed. The very air felt different, charged somehow with an energy and emotion she couldn't decipher. Her stomach cramped from exhaustion and far too many nerves. "I think this is our cue to leave. I have rooms booked at the Hotel Arcadia, and we'll return there now so Michael can be changed and have another bottle before taking his afternoon nap."

For a long moment there was silence, and then Gio leaned forward. "I think you should stay here."

She blinked, confused. "Here? Why?"

He rose and walked toward her. "You've started something, calling the paparazzi and inviting them here. You unleashed the wolves, and once they're out, they don't go away. They're circling, waiting for you—"

"You make it sound as if they're going to attack!"

"Because they will. And you're not going to be able to control them." He stopped in front of her, his gaze raking her first, and then the baby, who was contentedly gumming his fist. "It's not safe for you out there anymore."

Rachel's heart was racing, and not because he was frightening her, but standing this close she could feel his incredible physical energy as strongly as when he'd held her and kissed her outside in front of the cameras and anybody else watching. "They are photographers, not assassins."

"They might as well be assassins. They're not your friends. They'll want a piece of you, again and again."

"I'll keep that in mind."

"Then I'll send for your things from the Arcadia and we'll get you settled here—"

"No!"

He ignored her protest. "It's not safe for you out there. You can't be running around Venice, hopping in and out of water taxis with my nephew, and there is no need, either, when we can accomplish everything we need here, in privacy."

"I'm not…comfortable…staying here."

One of his black eyebrows lifted.

"It's your home, not mine," she said too quickly. "I'm not suggesting you'd be a poor host, but I would be a poor guest. I don't sleep well and I spend half the night pacing, unable to relax."

"But you will be able to relax here. You'll have help with the child—"

"Can you please stop calling him the child? His name is Michael. Michael Marcello."

"Michael Marcello Bern," he corrected. "I've seen the birth certificate. Your sister and my brother were not married, which is why Marcello has become a middle name instead of a surname."

"*This* is why I don't want to stay here," she said, looking away and biting down hard on her lower lip.

Instead of trying to meet her halfway, he was

sharp and negative, offering nothing but criticisms. He didn't want to see Michael as a real person. He didn't want to acknowledge Michael as someone of value. No, far better to make him a problem. Something to be discussed the way you'd discuss a bad business deal.

"He's a gorgeous boy, and he's inherited the Marcello coloring. I don't know if he looks like Antonio. I don't know what Antonio looked like as a baby, but he's lovely—"

"No one is criticizing him, and no one is locking you up, or taking your freedom away. But you need help—you've said so many times—and you'll get that help here."

She looked down into Michael's face. His big dark eyes looked up at her, his expression trusting and adoring. Her heart squeezed. She loved him. She'd become so attached to him and couldn't imagine life without him. "I don't want my old life back. He's…mine…now. But yes, help, would be nice. The *right* help that is."

"Then stay here where Michael can get lots of attention and you can rest."

Rachel drew a breath. "I really would be free to come and go? I could go for walks, or shopping?"

"As long as you don't take Michael, yes, as I am going to insist that he stays here, hidden and secure. I want to keep him from the cameras. What we discuss, and the decisions we make, should not be dictated by the media." He reached into his pocket and drew out his phone. "I'll send for Anna. She'll show you the way to the guest rooms on the fourth floor."

CHAPTER SIX

SHE'D BEEN TO Venice once before, and she'd loved the city then. It had been like a fantasy, an implausible city built on water with twisting streets and secret courtyards, whimsical arched bridges and mysterious exteriors that hid fairy-tale interiors.

She'd spent her entire visit wishing she could get lost inside one of the grand private homes lining the canals, exploring the historic palazzos, discovering the Venice that tourists never got to see. Four years later, she was back, a guest in one of the finest Venetian palazzos, and her guest suite took her breath away.

"Your room, Signorina Bern," Anna said, opening the tall wood shutters, allowing light to pour in.

Despite the gray gloomy day outside, the room glowed with color. The thick wood moldings and beamed ceiling were a lustrous gold, and the walls were covered in a fine blue silk the color of aquamarine above a teal and ivory marble wainscoting. A plush carpet in a brilliant blue with a gold and cream border nearly hid the dark hardwood floor, while the soaring four-poster canopy bed dominated the middle of the room, the posts completely hidden by opulent silk curtains and swags of fringed valances in the same gleaming aquamarine hue as the walls. The effect was dazzling, and would have been overwhelming if not for the crisp white bed coverlet and line of plump pillows against the blue painted headboard.

Anna pointed to the tall antique wardrobe with the mirrored doors. *"Il vostro guardaroba."* She struggled to remember her English. "For your clothes, yes?"

Rachel nodded, patting Michael's back. "Yes, thank you."

Then Anna crossed the room, moving to the center of the far wall, and opened the tall door, showing her through to a connected room where a gentleman was putting together a crib. "For the bambino."

It was another bedroom, smaller and far less opulent, the walls a pale shade of green, and the bed was smaller as well, anchored to the wall and featuring a cornice with green brocade fabric. The room was pretty and fresh with a pair of armchairs flanking the marble fireplace, but nothing like the grandeur of her room.

"Very nice," Rachel said, thinking it a lovely room, the colors reminding her of a nursery, but she didn't need Michael in a separate room. "But he could sleep in my room. His crib can be set up in mine."

Anna frowned. *"Non so quella parola."*

Rachel had no idea what the maid was saying and was too worn-out to try to make herself clear, when really, Michael's crib was not all that far, especially if she kept the door open between the rooms. She nodded, giving in.

Anna's gaze skimmed the baby's room and then the blue bedroom. She seemed satisfied with what she saw. *"Vorresti pranzo?"* she asked.

Rachel hated how stupid she felt. *"Pranzo?"*

Anna made the motion of feeding herself. "Eat. Lunch? *Pranzo*, yes?"

Actually Rachel was suddenly quite hungry. "Yes, please. Thank you."

As the door closed behind the maid, Rachel sat down with Michael in the blue velvet upholstered chair, and sighed, flattened. It had been quite the morning. Her head was spinning. She closed her eyes, and didn't open them until the knock at her door woke her.

Glancing down at Michael, she saw that he, too, was sleeping. She smiled a little and carefully rose, opening the door for Anna, who had brought her a lunch tray.

Anna positioned the tray on the small table next to the blue chair, shifting the small plates of crostini topped with truffle-laced cheese, prosciutto and whipped salted cod forward, leaving the bowl of salad behind, before opening the bottle of fizzy water and filling a glass for Rachel. "Thank you," Rachel said gratefully.

Gio entered the room as Anna slipped out. He was carrying Michael's diaper bag and he placed it on the foot of the bed.

Rachel was between bites. She slowly set the toast down and just looked at Gio, who seemed impossibly tall and imposing.

"Do you need anything?" he asked gruffly.

"I'm fine," she answered, giving a strained smile. "I've gotten quite adept at eating one-handed." But just then Michael shifted, stretching, and slid across her chest. She readjusted him and grimaced. "Perhaps adept isn't the right word, but we get by."

Giovanni's forehead creased. "Have you really had no help?"

"Friends will sometimes pop by, and when they do, I practically shove Michael into their arms before dashing off to shower and shampoo my hair."

"If I was one of your friends, I don't think I'd stop by very often."

She grinned ruefully. "They don't, not anymore. I think they've all realized I'll just put them to work…and then I'll disappear."

He stood in front of her, looking down at her, a crease between his strong black brows. "He looks very much like Antonio," he said after a long moment.

"I wondered," she answered.

Another uncomfortable beat of silence passed. "Hand him to me. My arms work, and you can eat."

Giovanni didn't have a lot of experience with babies. He hadn't thought about being a father since he ended his engagement to Adelisa. But seeing Michael nestle against Rachel's breast stirred something within him.

Love. Longing. Pain.

Not for his own children, but for this baby. Antonio's son.

He missed Antonio. He missed his best friend. Antonio had been warmth and humor, wit and charm. He'd balanced Gio and provided perspective. Just seeing the baby—Antonio's baby—made the grief more acute. Maybe it was because the baby also made Antonio real again.

In Michael, Antonio still lived.

Gio took the baby from Rachel and awkwardly settled him on his shoulder. Michael fussed a little, and then relaxed, back asleep.

The small body was warm. The infant's hand flexed and relaxed against Gio's neck. The feel of Michael's tiny fingers made the air trap in his lungs. His chest tightened—more sensation, more uncomfortable sensation.

Even without a DNA test, Giovanni was increasingly certain that Michael was Antonio's.

There was definitely something in the baby boy's face that reminded him of the Marcellos, and not just because the infant had a thatch of jet-black hair and the dark bright eyes. The six-month-old had a habit of pulling his brows, frowning in concentration, making himself look like a world-weary old man. It was something Antonio had always done, even as a very young child. He'd focus intently, thinking whatever he was thinking, and then when satisfied he'd smile.

The smile was Antonio.

The frown was Antonio.

Which meant, Michael belonged here in Venice. The Marcellos were Venetian. They didn't grow up in America, much less on the West Coast in a city like Seattle.

"Won't you miss him if you return to work?" Gio asked quietly.

"Yes," she answered, looking unhappy.

"Then stay home with him."

"But I have bills—"

"You've come to me for help. Let me help."

"How?"

"You wanted financial help. I'll give it."

"You'd pay my rent? And make my car payment? And give me an allowance for food and incidentals?" Her brows pulled. "I don't think so. I couldn't accept that. I don't want to be that dependent on anyone."

"Don't think of it that way. Think of it as earning a salary. Instead of paying for a nanny, I'd pay you."

"Which would make you my employer." Her cheeks flushed a dark pink. "No, thank you."

"But you need an employer."

"I have one. And it's a job I like very much, too. I need help paying for a nanny, that's all."

"But that's not all you need. You've made it clear that you want my family to be part of his life. You want us to ease some of the responsibility. So let us do that. Let me do that."

She pushed the tray back and rose. "I can take him now. I'm finished."

"No need. I have him. Why don't you relax?"

Her jaw tensed. She tried to smile but it was strained. "I'm sure you have things to do, whereas I have nothing."

"You could rest. Take a nap—"

"Can't. I don't really sleep anymore." But she did sit down again, and her hands folded in her lap. She was still smiling, but the smile was brittle. He saw for the first time the tension at her mouth and the shadows under her eyes.

"Is Michael sleeping?" Gio asked.

"He still wakes up at least once each night."

No wonder she was exhausted. "At what point do babies sleep through the night?"

"He should be able to sleep through the night

now. I'm afraid it's a habit he's developed. He doesn't drink much when he wakes up. He likes to socialize." Her lips pressed into a line. "I'm trying to convince him that daytime is much better for play."

"Perhaps I should hire a night nurse while you're here—"

"No! Don't do that. He'd be frightened. It's hard enough not being in his own bed, in his own room. Having a stranger care for him would surely confuse him."

"But what about you? Couldn't you use a night of uninterrupted sleep?"

"Yes, but I would feel guilty, and then I wouldn't sleep and it'd be a pointless exercise all the way around."

Gio glanced down into Michael's face and then at Rachel. "But if you hope to return to work, you need to get used to help. Soon you'll be away from him for eight hours or more a day."

He could see the misery in her eyes. She wasn't happy about that, either.

Gio gave her a long thoughtful look. "I'm glad you're here. It's time I did my part." He carefully eased the baby back into her arms. "We'll discuss this tonight. Let's meet for drinks in the library at seven. Signora Fabbro will stay with Michael."

"Mrs. Fabbro?" she repeated.

He nodded once and walked out.

* * *

Heart pounding, Rachel watched Gio leave, her insides a jittery mess.

Everything was changing. She could feel it. Once again her life was being upended.

But before she could sort out why she felt so uneasy, Anna arrived with Rachel's luggage. The maid wheeled in the large suitcase, and then removed the lunch tray.

Suddenly everything felt different—not just precarious, but overwhelming, and she didn't even understand what was changing.

While Anna insisted on unpacking the suitcase, Rachel placed Michael in the crib, and then she didn't know what to do with herself.

Jet lag didn't help anxiety, and right now her anxiety was at an all-time high. Sleep would help. Sleep always helped, but instead she paced the luxurious suite on the fourth floor of the palazzo, a fist pressed to her mouth as she chewed mindlessly on a knuckle, trying to ease the sick, heavy panicked sensation filling her middle.

She understood why Giovanni wanted her in his family palace. Notoriously private, he was trying to limit the media's access to Rachel and the baby. He was trying to protect his family name, and he wanted security and safeguards in place, but for her, it was suffocating. It was hard giving up her personal space, and she couldn't help feeling as if she'd lost her independence and control.

Control was important in this instance because she needed room to move and think.

Before lunch she would have said that she didn't think Gio knew the first thing about babies, and she'd thought his coldness had been due to inexperience with small children, but when he'd taken Michael from her, he'd handled his nephew with an easy confidence and almost affection.

What if Giovanni wanted to do more than provide financial assistance? What if Gio wanted Michael to stay in Venice?

The thought turned her insides into ice. She wasn't just accustomed to caring for Michael now, he was part of her. She loved him. She never used the words out loud, but she was his mother now. He was her son. If Giovanni challenged her for custody, Rachel would be in trouble. Juliet didn't have a living will. There had been no instructions for Michael, nothing to indicate her preference for guardianship.

Gio had a legitimate claim if he wanted to sue for custody.

She prayed he didn't want to be guardian. She prayed he didn't want to be responsible for a baby, because truthfully, she didn't want him making decisions about Michael's life or physical care. She just needed Giovanni's financial support so that once she and Michael were back in Seattle, she could hire a good sitter or nanny, buy the basic things a small person needed and move on with her life, a life as a single mother.

Mrs. Fabbro arrived at Rachel's door promptly at six-forty-five, announcing herself with a firm, loud knock.

Small and sturdy-looking, Mrs. Fabbro had steel-colored hair, shrewd dark eyes and a firm mouth that didn't seem likely to smile as she marched into the room. Introductions were awkward as her English was worse than Anna's and Rachel struggled in her limited Italian, but conversation was no longer an issue once Mrs. Fabbro spotted Michael in his fleecy pajamas on his blanket on the floor.

Rachel had placed him there so he wouldn't fall or get hurt while she dressed for dinner, and he seemed perfectly happy playing with his hands and kicking his legs in the air and just enjoying his freedom. But from Mrs. Fabbro's rapid Italian, the older woman didn't seem pleased to find her charge on the floor. She walked across the room and scooped him up from his blanket, crooning to him in Italian as if they were long-lost friends.

For a long moment Michael stared at Mrs. Fabbro, not sure whether she was friend or foe, but then his eyes crinkled and he grinned and put a wet fist on her chin.

"Bello raggazo," she said approvingly.

Michael chortled, and Mrs. Fabbro put him on

her hip for the tour of the rooms. "His bed is in here," Rachel said, walking into the adjoining room that had obviously been a sitting room before someone added the crib.

"His bottle is here," she added, pointing to the sideboard, where she'd laid out his bottles and formula. "One bottle before bed, and then I burp him and put him down. He sleeps on his back, no covers, or toys with him."

She'd already made a bottle so it would be ready, but she made a second one up, just so the woman could see how they were made. "Do you have any questions?" Rachel asked.

Mrs. Fabbro shook her head and took Michael's hand and helped him wave bye-bye before taking him on a walk around his room.

Rachel was now free to finish preparing for dinner but she stood a moment in the doorway watching the older woman talk to Michael and point things out, giving him his first lessons in Italian.

Rachel's eyes stung, and she blinked back the prickle of tears. She wasn't sure why she suddenly felt so emotional. She ought to be happy that Mrs. Fabbro was efficient and quick to take charge of Michael, but Michael had been her responsibility long enough that without him, she felt painfully empty.

Things had been chaotic and stressful for months, and it was only recently that she'd begun to feel more settled and comfortable as Michael's mom. They'd begun to find a rhythm, and they'd created a schedule that helped them both, and she understood that it was her and Michael together now. She understood that it would probably always be just the two of them, at least in terms of them as a nuclear family.

If only she could take Michael with her to drinks and dinner. She'd feel better. Safer. Michael was a good distraction. Whenever she'd felt too much earlier, she'd patted Michael's back and kissed his sweet soft cheek, and he'd helped calm her. But tonight she wouldn't have Michael as a buffer. It would just be Giovanni and her. Alone.

Rachel returned to the tall painted wardrobe where she'd hung up the two dresses she'd brought. The rest were trousers and sweaters and coats, winter wear appropriate for Venice's chilly wet weather. The dresses were ones she might have worn to a business dinner, a long-sleeved black velvet sheath dress with a V-neckline, or a chocolate-colored lace dress with cap sleeves and a tiered skirt that went from high to low, with the shortest ruffle at her knees and then the longest touching the ground.

She'd brought the dresses thinking that maybe there would be a dinner with Giovanni Marcello, imagining he might invite her and Michael to his home one evening, or maybe to meet at a local restaurant, but being here was nothing like she'd imagined. She felt so unsettled, so nervous.

Aware that she'd soon be late, she quickly slipped into her black velvet dress and pulled her hair back into a loose chignon before slipping into heels and reaching for a dark gray velvet wrap with a pretty black and silver beaded fringe. It had been her great-grandmother's, and even though it was a vintage nineteen-twenties shawl, it still looked exquisite and just a little bit well-loved, but perfect for a night like tonight when Rachel needed confidence.

The elderly butler from the morning was waiting on the third landing for Rachel and he walked her slowly down the hall. The butler gravely opened the door and stepped back, and Rachel entered the Marcello library, a windowless room where the walls were covered in antique ruby brocade paper and narrow gilded bookshelves rivaled massive oil paintings. The center of the room was filled with oversize crimson sofas and thickly padded upholstered armchairs, pieces promising comfort and not just style.

Rachel spotted Gio across the room, dressed in a dark suit and white dress shirt. He looked immaculate and handsome—far, far too handsome—and it suddenly struck her as odd that he hadn't ever married. He was a man who had everything. Why was he still a bachelor in his late thirties?

* * *

Giovanni turned at the sound of the door quietly closing. He'd been pouring a drink and he straightened when he spotted Rachel hesitating on the threshold. She looked different this evening. Younger, softer, a little less sure of herself.

Earlier today she'd reminded him of Adelisa, but tonight she was just Rachel, and he didn't know if it was due to the simplicity of her black velvet dress, or perhaps the way she'd styled her hair, the long thick strands twisted and pinned at the back of her neck in a style that struck him as Edwardian. Even her dress and shawl had a hint of old-world elegance. Maybe that was the difference. She looked pretty and fresh without being overdone.

"I'm sorry for being late," she said a little breathlessly.

He shook his head. "Not late."

"I think I am, by about ten minutes."

"It's just an *aperitivo*, a predinner drink. Our schedule is not set in stone." He nodded at the tray with the crystal decanters and glasses. "What can I pour for you?"

"Do you have any wine, or is that not a suitable *aperitivo*?"

He smiled faintly. "Sparkling wine is definitely suitable. Would you prefer Prosecco, Fragolino, or perhaps Brachetto?"

She moved slowly toward him, expression shy.

"Are they all wine? Will you think me terribly gauche when I say I don't know the difference?"

"They're all wine with bubbles. And does my opinion matter? Earlier today you said you didn't care what I thought of you."

Her shoulders twisted. "I was feeling defensive earlier."

"And you aren't now?"

"I've had a chance to nap and relax, and gain a little more perspective."

"And what is that?"

"If we're to be allies, not adversaries, we need to get along, right?"

For a long moment he just looked at her. "We shall see what you have to say after I show you the papers."

"What's in the papers?"

"Let's have that drink first." He saw her quick glance, and the worry in her brown eyes. She wouldn't like what she saw. He wasn't surprised at the newspapers. It's what he'd intended, but it changed everything. For him. For her. For all of them.

"It sounds as if a quick lesson is in order," he said casually. "Prosecco is Italian, it's a sparkling wine made here in Veneto from Glera grapes. Fragolino is a sparkling red wine, also made in the Veneto, from the Isabella grape, while Brachetto, also a sparkling red, comes from the Piedmont region." He looked at her. "What sounds good?"

She wrinkled her nose. "Too many choices."

"Let us simplify. Red or white?"

"White, please."

"Prosecco it is." He opened a bottle and filled a flute for her. "I think you made a good choice. This comes from the Marcello vineyard."

"You have a winery?"

"It's a small one, but I'm proud of it. The wines are beginning to win awards and receive international recognition."

"Are you very involved?"

"I bought the ailing vineyard six years ago. We're just starting to turn a profit. Winemaking is a labor of love. You don't do it to get rich."

"Is the Marcello vineyard your labor of love?"

"More than I expected."

"Now I'm even more embarrassed that I knew nothing about Italian wine."

"I don't pretend to be a vintner. I'm an engineer. I build things."

She took the flute from him, and then looked up into his eyes. "I'd like to see the papers. You have me worried now."

He walked her to the long table behind the couch. He'd cleared the table of everything but the newspapers and pages he'd printed from various digital media sites.

Every story ran with one or more photos, and every story had a shot of Rachel with Michael, but there were far more photographs of Rachel in Giovanni's arms than of Michael himself. The baby was a secondary story to Giovanni Marcello passionately kissing the mother of his child.

He watched Rachel lean over the table to get a better look at the different pages, her lashes lowering as she scanned the headlines, and then glanced over the photos. As she studied the papers, color suffused her cheeks, turning her pale ivory skin to a hot pink.

"I can't read the headlines since they seem to be in every language but English," she said quietly. "Can you please translate for me?"

"'Marcello's Love-Child! Gio Marcello's Secret Affair! Mystery Mistress and Mother to His Child! Is This the Marcello Heir?'"

As he read the translated headlines to her, the pink color receded, leaving her face pale. "Is there no mention of Antonio? Do they all think that the baby is yours?"

"They all seem to think that Michael is ours."

"But I told them the baby was the Marcello heir—" She broke off, lips tightening. She gave her dark head a shake, the coiled knot at her nape glossy in the soft lighting. "The kiss. That changed everything, didn't it?" She looked up at him, frustration etched on her face. "You said it would, and you were right."

"I had to control the story."

"But we're not a couple, and he's not our child, which makes every bit of this a lie!"

"The tabloids don't care. They just want to sell copies and increase their advertising."

She began to quickly stack the pages. "Thankfully these are not stories on the front page of the papers," she said, irritably. "And these are not serious newspapers—"

"Well, two of the papers are national newspapers. The story and photos are not on the front page, but placed inside the lifestyle and society pages."

Papers stacked, she folded them in half, and then folded them again, hiding all the headlines and incriminating photos. Once she'd finished hiding the headlines, she reached for her flute and gulped the fizzy white wine as if she, too, could disappear into the crisp bubbles. "No one will take me seriously at work if this story gets traction." She shot him a desperate look. "You must smash this story, before I no longer have a job."

"You were the one that contacted the media. You started this."

"I didn't start this, I shared the truth. Facts—"

"Facts that could wreck the Marcello name and reputation. I couldn't have that."

"But my name and reputation doesn't matter?"

"One's reputation always matters, but you've far less invested in your name and brand than I do."

"No, I'm not a billionaire. No, I don't head up a huge corporation. But my name is also very important. Maybe not to you, but it is to me." She exhaled hard. "I'm going to correct them."

"We're not going to correct them. This is what I wanted."

"Even though the stories are false?"

"We know that, but the public doesn't, and in this instance, fiction is preferable, because these are headlines we can shape and control."

CHAPTER SEVEN

RACHEL SET HER half-empty flute down and walked away. She'd only had a couple of sips but the wine was going to her head, making her emotional, which of course didn't make it easier to think.

It was also easier to be logical when she wasn't standing close to Giovanni. He was too beautiful, too much like a model she might have admired in the pages of a glossy magazine with his high cheekbones and strong chin and firm mouth that kissed far too well. He had a face that made her melt, but unlike Antonio who was laid-back and friendly, Giovanni was hard and reserved. Shuttered. He exuded intensity, confidence and power, things she could handle when sitting at a conference table or on the phone in a long-distance call, but not close to her, not when Giovanni made the power feel physical, masculine, sensual.

Even now, standing across the room, she could still feel him, his energy hot and simmering, electrifying the room. Electrifying her.

She didn't think she'd ever met a man who'd

filled a room the way he did, owning the air and space, swallowing all the oxygen so that she couldn't breathe.

Most troubling of all was that a small part of her had almost enjoyed the intensity, and that same part of her was humming with awareness. She'd never admit it to anyone but she'd been drawn to his energy and the shimmering heat surrounding him—even though the heat and energy could obliterate her.

Her brain was warning her off, telling her that he was too much for her. Too hard, too confident, too dangerous. Her practical side understood that he didn't care for her, and that he wouldn't protect her, that nothing good would come of allowing herself to be intrigued by him.

But she was already intrigued. She was fascinated and curious and drawn to him…

Standing next to him moments ago, she wanted him to touch her again. She'd wanted him to reach for her and cover her mouth with his and make her feel what she'd felt earlier.

If that wasn't crazy, she didn't know what was.

No, crazy was the fact that she didn't like him, or admire him, and yet she still wanted him to touch her again. She wanted to feel more. Even now, with sofas and tables and armchairs between them, she was still responding to him, the very thought of him kissing her again making her shiver inwardly, making her ache.

"Why do you want the paparazzi to think the baby is ours?" she asked, her voice low and husky.

"It's simpler."

"It's actually not. It is going to be far more work trying to convince people that we were a couple and we had a baby—"

"They already believe it."

"But I don't like that story!" Heat rushed through her, the heat so strong that her skin prickled and burned.

"I don't like it, either, but given our choices, it's the better one."

"Why? *How?*"

"This version deflects attention away from Antonio and Juliet. We can protect and preserve their memory, allowing the mistakes of the past to fade—"

"Antonio and Juliet had a baby. Why is that such a travesty?"

"They weren't married, or even serious. It was a brief affair, a sexual fling—"

"I disagree. Juliet loved your brother, deeply."

"I'm sure she wanted to be convincing."

"She really did care, Giovanni."

He shrugged. "Maybe as much as she could care, but either way, she was ultimately selfish and destructive and not someone I want associated with my family."

Rachel recoiled. "That is incredibly harsh," she breathed, putting a hand to her middle, trying to calm herself, not easy when her stomach did wild flips. Juliet hadn't been an angel. She didn't have many altruistic bones in her body, and yet she wasn't the devil incarnate. She'd been complicated and had had aspirations—aspirations Rachel didn't understand—but when all was said and done, she was her sister, her younger sister, and it was painful to hear Giovanni's brutal denouncement. "You met her then?" she asked.

"No. But I know a great deal about her, and women like her."

His scathing tone made her see red. Her chin jerked up. "Juliet loved him—"

"There was no love. I can promise you that." Gio's light blue eyes narrowed, his full mouth firming. He looked hard and darkly handsome, arrogant and utterly unapproachable. "Your sister saw her opportunity to make a fortune and took advantage of the situation."

"I am absolutely certain Juliet didn't know he was ill. *I* didn't know he was ill, and I was the one that introduced them."

"*You're* responsible."

She thought for a moment he was joking, or teasing, but there was no softening of his features, or flicker of warmth in his eyes. "Do you need to blame someone? If so, yes, blame me. It's all my fault. I did it. The love affair, the pregnancy, the tragic loss of two beautiful people—"

"You're not helping."

"I'm not helping? What about you? Have you no responsibility at all, to anything other than your business, and your name, and protecting your brand? You say my sister was selfish—well, you are every bit as calculating and self-serving. It's a shame you didn't meet her. You and Juliet would have been a perfect match!"

"You are not that innocent, Rachel. You have played a significant part in this drama."

"Did I? How fascinating."

"I'd use the word despicable, rather than fascinating, and it makes me wonder how many other men did you introduce her to? How many of your clients did she date?"

"That has no bearing on Juliet and Antonio's relationship."

"I think it does. You were her matchmaker, weren't you? You'd introduce her to your wealthy clients, helping her to land a rich husband."

"I never played matchmaker. Not once. Antonio and Juliet met because your brother and I were out discussing the plane delivery schedule over a drink and she walked in, and so yes, I introduced them, but it wasn't planned."

"So she never dated any other of your clients? And think carefully about your answer, as your credibility is on the line. You weren't the only one to hire a private investigator. I know all about her *dating* history."

Rachel drew a rough breath, shaken. "What do you mean?"

"She'd been on the hunt for a rich man for years, and she used you fairly frequently for introductions—"

"It may have happened once or twice, but it was by chance. I never set out to introduce her to any of my customers. It was always by accident."

"You expect me to believe that?" He crossed the room, closing the distance in long livid strides. "Come on. Be serious. Tell me how it really worked. Did you get a percentage? Were you ever offered a piece of the action?"

She backed up into a bookshelf, and then could go no farther. "How can you say such a thing? What is wrong with you?"

"It struck me just now that you are part of the game. I suspected it—"

"You're wrong. I'm not playing a game. There is no game. There is just a baby boy that needs our help." She drew a short sharp breath, face hot, her heart hammering so hard she felt like throwing up. He was awful. Beyond awful. "Good night," she choked, putting down her glass and racing from the room to climb the white Carrera marble stairs as quickly as she could.

She heard Gio's oath as he followed.

She ran faster, but his legs were longer and he reached her just before she reached the next floor, his hand circling her wrist, stopping her progress. She teetered on her heels.

He put his hand on her waist, turning her around. "Where are you going? What are you doing?" he growled.

She was out of breath and close to tears. "I'm not going to stand there and listen to you make ugly accusations. You have a twisted view of the world, and I refuse to be dragged into—"

His head dropped, his mouth covering hers, silencing the words. She stiffened, but he pulled her closer. Her lips parted to protest and she tasted the warm sweet wine on his breath and could smell his fragrance and the mixture was delicious. He smelled delicious.

Funny how she disliked Giovanni so much and yet she loved his kisses...

He made her feel beautiful and desirable, and in his arms, with his mouth on hers, his body pressed against her, she felt wonderfully alive. Almost too alive. Fire streaked through her veins, making her hum.

She'd always felt this way on the inside, deep down, but no one had ever brought it out in her, or seen her as anything but practical and pragmatic. And cold.

But she wasn't cold. Her feelings were strong and they went so deep. She'd spent her life trying to hide the intensity of those emotions, but

Giovanni had somehow discovered them and he knew just how to use them against her.

She didn't know if he felt her shudder, but he drew her even closer, his lips parting hers, his tongue caressing the softness of her lower lip, and then stroking deeper, sweeping her mouth, electrifying her nerve endings, making them dance.

Was it terrible that she liked the way he touched her? That she welcomed his arm around her waist and his hand sliding low on her hip?

She welcomed the crush of his chest and the sinewy strength of his legs. He was hard and commanding, and nothing had ever felt so exciting, or quite so right.

No kiss had ever felt so good. She felt good. Brilliant, and beautiful, and fiercely alive, tingling everywhere. It wasn't real; it couldn't be real. Men loved Juliet, not her. Juliet fascinated men with her physical perfection. And Rachel was so far from perfect...

The thought stopped her, ending the magic, reminding her of who she was, and who he was, and why he was here.

She pulled back, breathing heavily, body still exquisitely sensitive, to look up at Gio. "We shouldn't do this." She struggled to speak, her voice low and hoarse. "It won't help."

He stared down at her, his brilliant eyes studying her intently, taking in every inch of her face before reaching out to trace one of her eyebrows and then the other. *"Bella donna."*

She blinked, unable to think of anything but the stroke of his finger along the arch of her brow. It felt good to be touched. Everything inside her was warm and aching, tingling with need. She'd forgotten that she could feel need. And desire.

Maybe that's why the desire was so strong. Maybe she'd gone too long without feeling anything, and now she was feeling, and it was intense. Her entire body trembled. Her lashes closed as he caressed her jaw, his thumb stroking along the jawbone and then over the fullness of her mouth. Waves of pleasure rippled through her and she couldn't suppress the shudders. It was embarrassing, feeling so much, wanting to be kissed and touched and pleasured.

She swallowed hard and opened her eyes, her gaze locking with Gio's. His eyes were hot, bright, and the intensity in the depths burned her. He wanted her, too.

It was a heady realization and it rocked her, bumping up against her confidence, or lack of. She could maybe pass as a decent kisser but she wasn't experienced, and she didn't have the first idea how to please a man.

Furthermore, she shouldn't be thinking of how to please a man if that man was Michael's uncle, billionaire Giovanni Marcello.

"We'll both regret this tomorrow," she said,

keeping a hand on his arm because she didn't trust her legs, or her balance. "It'll make the discussions more difficult."

"You were the one that said it would be better if we liked each other."

"I didn't mean physically."

"You can love a child, and still be a beautiful woman."

"I don't have affairs and flings, Gio. I'm not looking for a relationship, either."

"But you don't have a boyfriend."

"Heavens, no," she choked, face hot. "I'd never kiss you if I did, and I haven't had a relationship in years." It was more than that. She hadn't ever had a serious boyfriend or a first lover, but she wouldn't confess the entire truth. It'd be too mortifying if he knew.

"Why not?"

"For the same reason you prefer to live here, instead of Rome. I'm a solitary creature. I like my space."

"Even though I barely know you, I have to say I don't believe you." He ran a fingertip over her cheekbone and then around her ear. "You strike me as someone who very much needs people. Provided they are the right people."

She was lost, looking into his eyes. He was right. She did need people, good people. It was hard being responsible for everyone and everything. Hard having to be the grown-up, from a very young age. But she'd rather be the grown-up and do the right thing, than be impulsive and hurt Michael and the need for stability in his future. "I agree with you," she said, drawing away. "But I also know that you aren't one of those people for me."

He gave her a look she couldn't decipher. "I'm not in the habit of arguing with women."

"Good."

"But I'm going to prove you wrong."

Her heart did a funny little flutter that made her breathless and hurt all at the same time. "Please don't. I'm only here for a few days. Let's focus on Michael. He's what's important." She climbed one step and then another until she reached the landing, and then paused to look down at Giovanni. Her heart did another painful beat. "Tomorrow let's sort this out for his sake, please. I need to return to Seattle."

"Is that the best thing for Michael? Or the best thing for you?"

She frowned. "It's the best thing for both of us."

"I'm not sure anymore that it is."

Her heart fell. She was right. He was changing his mind. He wanted Michael to stay here. He wanted Michael in Venice. Her eyes stung and her throat ached.

Before she broke down in tears, or said something she'd regret, Rachel fled.

* * *

Gio stood on the marble stair and watched Rachel disappear down the hallway, her footsteps practically flying in her need to escape.

He exhaled shortly. Tonight had not gone as planned, and what had taken place in the library, that was wrong. He knew he was at fault, too. The entire scene weighed on him. His stomach felt like he'd been chewing on rocks and glass.

He didn't understand how he'd lost control of the situation so fast, and so completely. One minute they were discussing the newspaper headlines, and the next they were battling about ambitious Juliet whom Giovanni loathed, and then somehow Rachel was part of the fight and at the receiving end of his frustration and fury.

He didn't actually believe Rachel was Juliet's matchmaker, and he certainly didn't think she'd benefited in any way from Juliet's schemes, but Juliet was as amoral as they came. To pursue a dying man? To deliberately get pregnant, not caring that you were creating a life where the child would never know his or her own father?

Gio was far from perfect. As Rachel had said, he was driven and ambitious, but there had to be a line one didn't cross. Juliet had no such scruples, and she'd needlessly complicated Antonio's final year, creating pain not just for Antonio, but the whole family.

But tonight his frustration wasn't with Juliet. It was with himself.

Why was he so intent on provoking Rachel? Why did he want to test her, tease her, draw a response from her?

What did he want from her?

But that was actually easy. What *didn't* he want from her?

She'd woken him, and the desire consumed him. It had been far too long since he'd felt emotion, or hunger, and he felt both now.

He wanted her. And he would have her.

CHAPTER EIGHT

HE'D GONE TO bed tense, and then woke in the middle of the night to the sound of a baby crying.

It wasn't an ear-piercing cry, but more fretful and prolonged. Giovanni rolled onto his back, smashing his pillow behind his head, and listened, eyes closed, to the wail coming from down the hall, realizing that he'd heard the crying even in his sleep and had incorporated the sound in his dream.

It hadn't been a pleasant dream, either. He'd been talking with Antonio and they'd argued, and he didn't remember what they were arguing about but it was tense, and Antonio turned around to face him, and as he turned the baby was there in his arms. And then the baby was crying, and Antonio blamed him for upsetting Michael, and Giovanni answered that he'd done nothing and that's when he woke up.

And heard the baby crying down the hall in his room.

Was no one going to the baby? Could Rachel not hear him? Or had something happened to Rachel?

Giovanni flipped the covers back and climbed from the bed, throwing his robe on over his pajama bottoms. The pale green room was dimly lit, illuminated only by a small night-light. In the soft yellow glow he could see Rachel holding Michael and patting his back, crooning in his ear but the baby cried on, miserable.

She was facing the oil landscape on the wall, gently jiggling the baby as she studied the scene, unaware that she was being watched. She really was good with Michael, he thought, very much the mother the baby needed.

They would both stay here with him, he decided. It was logical. It made sense. Michael needed Rachel, and Giovanni wanted both Michael and Rachel…

"Is this normal?" he asked, approaching them.

She startled, turning quickly to face him. "He's teething. It makes him fretful. But he's not settling down and he feels warm to me. He might be coming down with something, which would explain why he's been not quite himself the past few days."

"He's running a fever?"

"I think so."

"You haven't checked?"

She gave him a look he couldn't decipher. "I didn't bring a thermometer with me, but I'll go buy one in the morning. You must have a pharmacy nearby, and if he's feverish, I'll take him to the doctor and have him checked out, just in case." She pressed her lips to the top of the baby's head. "Sorry to have disturbed you but we're fine."

She turned her back on him as she walked away, pacing back across the room, crooning in the fretful baby's ear. In her pink robe, with her hair loose over her shoulders, she was small and delicate and very, *very* appealing.

His body hardened. He wanted her—in his bed, and out of bed. But she was wary of him, almost skittish. "Do you want me to take a turn with him?" he offered. "Could you use a break?"

"I'm fine."

"You always say that."

"Because I am fine."

"Even when you're desperate, you're fine?"

She laughed softly. "I try very hard not to be hysterical. I don't enjoy the state of desperation."

Rachel blinked when Giovanni laughed, the sound low and husky. It was the first time she'd heard him laugh without mockery, and there was something in his voice, something in his amusement that thrilled her, making her flush with pleasure, her skin tingling, her body responding. It took so little for him to wake her up, make her come alive.

"You have a sense of humor," he said.

"Not according to my mother." But her lips

curved wryly. "She thought I needed a sense of humor, at least when it came to Juliet."

"How so?"

"I think she expected me to enjoy Juliet's adventures and triumphs more. Instead I was me. Difficult, prickly porcupine Rachel." She tried to smile again, but it felt tight and uncomfortable. "And to be fair, I wasn't amused by Juliet. She was a lot of work and demanded a lot of Mother's time. Or maybe Mother just preferred to focus on Juliet. Juliet was the beautiful daughter after all, and charming and admired by many. It gave my mother great pleasure to show her off."

"Was your mother beautiful?"

"No. She looked like me."

"You are beautiful."

Rachel sputtered. "Hardly. I'm fairly utilitarian, but that's okay. I've had twenty-eight years to come to terms with my attractiveness, or lack of—"

"Are you being serious?"

"Yes, and I don't want compliments. I don't need them. But I have a mirror, and a phone. I'm on social media. I know what beautiful is, and I know what society likes—"

"Society!" he scoffed. "And social media? You allow such things to influence you?"

"I know what's beautiful. Classical features. High cheekbones. Full, plumped lips. Flawless skin. I don't have any of that. My nose is too long, my mouth is too wide, my jaw is too strong, my eyes are a little too close—" She flushed, appalled that she'd said so much.

"I don't agree with you. Not at all."

"I'm not surprised. We don't agree on almost anything." She turned away, walking with Michael to the curtained window. She'd pushed the heavy silk drapes open earlier so she could see out. The tall houses across the narrow canal were dark but streetlights illuminated the sidewalk and cast a reflecting glimmer on the water. Venice looked so mysterious at night, with its labyrinth of canals and bridges, arches and hidden squares. It would be fun to explore the city at night, maybe even take one of those touristy ghost tours. Not that she wanted to encounter any ghosts.

"Are you really in danger of losing your job?" he asked, breaking the silence.

Rachel drew a slow breath, and then nodded. "I've used up all my sick days and vacation days, floating days and every unpaid leave day I could take. But management wants me back, or they need to hire someone else."

"Would you really miss work if they let you go?"

She glanced at him over her shoulder. "I love planes. I really like my job. It's exciting to be in the same field as my father. Admittedly, I'm not an aeronautical engineer, but I have his same passion for flight…it's exhilarating."

"So you really don't want me to support you. You don't want to stay home."

She hesitated. "Does that make me a bad woman?"

"Of course not."

"Did your mother work?"

"No." He laughed, a low mocking sound. "Her job was to look beautiful and spend money. She did both, quite well."

"Have any of your girlfriends worked?"

He took his time answering, and when he did, he was brief. "I don't really have girlfriends."

"No? What do you have?"

"Mistresses."

"How does a mistress differ from a girlfriend?"

"There is no emotional entanglement. It's a physical relationship." As if reading her confusion, he added bluntly. "I don't love them. And they don't love me."

"What do they get out of the relationship then, besides sex?"

"Great sex. And gifts."

Her brows arched. "That sounds horrible. Have there been many?"

His mouth curved, a crooked mocking smile. "I'm in my late thirties. So yes, there have been many."

"What are they like? Do you have a type?"

He leaned against the wall, hands buried in the robe pockets. The robe was pulling open, revealing the hard, muscular plane of his chest and a hint of his carved, chiseled torso. "I make it a point not to discuss past relationships."

She forced her attention from his incredibly fit body to his ruggedly handsome face. "I suspect it's not because you're protecting them, but because you don't like remembering. For you, there is no point in remembering. What's done is done. What's gone is gone."

Gio's black brow lifted. "You presume to know me?"

She shrugged. "You're an engineer. I work with engineers every day. You're all excessively practical."

"Next thing I know you'll be saying we lack imagination."

"Not so. You have excellent imaginations. If you didn't, how would you problem-solve? You have to imagine something to be able to build it."

"You fascinate me, *bella*."

"I doubt that very much."

His gaze met hers and held. He looked at her so intently that he made her grow warm all over again.

"I like smart women," he said quietly. "I like successful women. I wouldn't say I have a type but I am drawn to brunettes with interesting faces—

mouths that are generous, noses that aren't too short or small, jaws that aren't weak."

Heat rushed through her, even as her stomach turned inside out.

She didn't know where to look, or what to do. Spellbound, she stared across the room at a man who was absolutely larger than life and beyond anything she could have imagined for her. There was no reason he should like her, or be fascinated by her.

When little spots appeared before her eyes she realized she needed to breathe, and she dragged in a breath, dizzy, and dazed.

He couldn't possibly be serious, and yet he didn't seem to be laughing at her, or mocking her. He wasn't even smiling.

No, he looked very hard and very virile and far too self-assured. What she wouldn't give to have that kind of confidence.

Heart hammering, she glanced down at the baby in her arms. Michael had finally fallen asleep, his plump cheek pressed to her breast, his thumb against his mouth. He was so sweet, so beautiful. She loved him so much.

"He's out," she said. "I think he'll sleep the rest of the night without any more tears."

"That's good."

"It is," she agreed, kissing the baby again before crossing to his crib. Bending over, she carefully placed him on his back. In his sleep, Michael sighed and stretched, tiny fingers opening and then relaxing. She watched him a moment, suffused with so many different emotions. Love, tenderness, worry, hope.

Across the room she heard a soft click. Rachel looked up only to discover that Gio was gone.

Rachel woke up to a still dark room that was quiet and cool. Far too quiet and cool. Glancing to the door separating her room from Michael's, she saw that it was closed. Throwing back the covers, she raced from bed to yank the door open. The curtains had been drawn and the room was filled with a watery light. She'd taken several steps into the green room when she spotted Mrs. Fabbro walking past the tall arched windows, talking away to Michael in Italian, while Michael babbled back, as if the two were deep in conversation.

Rachel's pulse still pounded, and yet her lips curved into a faint smile.

Michael seemed to adore the older Italian woman.

Mrs. Fabbro spotted Rachel. *"Buongiorno,"* she said, nodding her gray head.

"Is it very late?" Rachel asked.

Mrs. Fabbro didn't seem to understand the question, but she crossed to the wall, and pressed a button. *"Signor Marcello vi aspetta."*

Rachel didn't understand Mrs. Fabbro, either. She walked over and held her hands out, gesturing that she'd like to take the baby.

Mrs. Fabbro seemed most reluctant to hand Michael over, but after a hesitation, she did.

Rachel nuzzled Michael's warm cheek. He smelled sweet and fresh. He must have had a bath this morning. "Has he eaten?" she asked. "Uh… *Bottiglia di latte?*" she stammered, trying to remember the words for bottle, or milk."

"Si. Due."

"He has." Gio's deep male voice came from behind her. "Two."

"Two?" Rachel said. "He never drinks that much when he wakes up."

"It's nearly noon. He's been up for hours."

Her jaw dropped. "I had no idea. I can't believe I slept that long."

"I told everyone you weren't to be disturbed, and Signora Fabbro has enjoyed her time with Michael. You're going to find it difficult to keep him out of her arms. She loves babies and children. She hates it when they grow up."

"Did she come with good references?"

"The best. She was Antonio's and my nanny." His expression softened as he looked at her. "I didn't tell her Michael was Antonio's until today. But I couldn't deny it when she asked."

"She guessed?"

"She knew he had to be mine, or his. He's very much a Marcello."

"You see the resemblance?"

"I do."

"Are you still going to run another DNA test?"

"It won't change the outcome, will it?"

Rachel shook her head.

"You used a reputable company for the testing. It's a company I've used before—" He frowned, a crease forming between his strong black brows.

"You must be hungry."

His abrupt change of subject made Rachel curious. What else was he going to say? "You've done DNA testing before, then?"

"It's getting close to lunch. We should talk, after we've eaten."

He wasn't going to tell her, was he? Rachel hugged Michael, savoring his sweetness, and the light clean scent from his baby shampoo. "I can't think of food until I have my coffee."

"Are you a big coffee drinker?"

"I live in Seattle. We like our coffee." The baby clearly didn't want to be held so tightly. He wiggled and pushed back against her chest. Smiling, Rachel loosened her hold. "He's feisty this morning. He's definitely feeling better."

Mrs. Fabbro now held her hands out, wanting to take Michael back. Her thin lips weren't smiling and the expression in her dark eyes was somewhat intimidating.

"She really was your nanny?" Rachel asked, glancing from Mrs. Fabbro to Gio.

Gio grinned. For a split second he looked boy-ish and young. "She was," he answered, still smil-ing. "She spoiled us rotten. She's a pussycat. Don't let her stern expression fool you."

Rachel handed the squirming baby over and Mrs. Fabbro triumphantly marched away, putting distance between them. Rachel watched her walk off. "She didn't need to send for you."

"She rang for Anna. I happened to be closer." Gio was also watching Mrs. Fabbro and Michael. "You don't need to worry about him, not with her. She couldn't have children of her own. Antonio and I became hers. She was very close to Anto-nio, so close that when he opened his own home in Florence, she went to oversee the house for him. She was still in his employ when he died." Gio's expression shifted, hardening. "After his death, I tried to bring her here, but she wouldn't leave his house. She's only here now because we finally closed his Florence villa and there was nowhere else to go."

It was a terribly sad story, Rachel thought, but also reassuring to hear that even as adults, the Marcello brothers had taken such good care of their nanny, and that she loved them so much in return. It was the kind of bond that spoke of af-fection rather than obligation.

It also made her realize she was going to have to fight Mrs. Fabbro for time with Michael.

"I'll have coffee sent to your room while you

change," Gio said. "And then once you're dressed, come to my office for lunch. I can share with you the latest newspapers and headlines, and then we can discuss what we're going to do."

CHAPTER NINE

RACHEL SCANNED THE newspapers spread out on the table in the living room adjoining Gio's study. There were many, too, and in a half-dozen different languages, today, including English.

"Everyone loves scandal," she said under her breath.

He heard her, though. "And sex," he added. "Sex sells."

She glanced across the table, and his expression was bland, but he looked relaxed and perfectly at ease, lounging back in his chair as if they were enjoying a leisurely lunch on a sunny terrace instead of a tense meal on a gloomy winter day.

"We didn't have sex, though," she corrected.

Gio shrugged. "Maybe we should."

She blushed furiously, not expecting that. "Can we stay on topic, please?"

"I am."

"No, that wasn't appropriate."

"It is, if we marry."

Her head jerked up. She stared at him in horror. Why say something like that? Why mock her?

"This isn't a game, Gio, and clearly my sense of humor is subpar, because I'm not enjoying your jokes—"

"I'm not playing games, *bella*, and I'm not one for jokes. I suggest marriage because it saves us from scandal, stealing the power from the media and giving it back to us. They don't drive the story—we do."

Rachel's brain couldn't keep up. She couldn't get past the "I suggest marriage" part. "I'm not even listening—"

"But you should," he said, leaning across the table to take her chin, forcing her head up to look her in the eyes. "Your timing could not be worse. One of Marcello SpA's companies is going public in just a few weeks. We've spent the past year preparing for this. My management team filed to IPO ten weeks ago and we're hoping to be trading in two weeks. It all looked very good, but this… circus you've created will reflect badly on my family, the company and going public."

"I didn't create a circus—"

"You brought the media here," he ground out, cutting her short.

She pulled away and leaned back in her chair, heart thumping, mouth drying. She had brought the media here, but she did it because he'd refused to speak to her or respond to her. She'd done what needed to be done. "I had no idea that you were trying to take a company public," she said quietly. "My coming here now wasn't about you, but trying to get Michael child care so I could return to work before I derail my career. There's nothing left in my checking account. My credit cards can't handle any more debt. I'm here because it's a matter of survival."

He said nothing, his expression grim and unforgiving.

She clasped her hands tightly together in her lap. She hated being weak, hated needing anything from others, having long prided herself on her independence, but Juliet's death had changed everything. "I said this before, and I mean it. If I had the means to take care of Michael on my own, I wouldn't be here. I didn't want to come to you. I would have preferred to raise him on my own, but I don't earn enough to cover a nanny and my bills. Furthermore, I love my job, and if it weren't for the new vice president of marketing, I wouldn't be here now. But he's decided to tighten up my department and he's not interested in excuses or conflicts or personal problems. If I'm not there on Monday, I'm not to return, ever."

The silence was heavy and suffocating. It seemed to stretch forever, too.

Finally, Giovanni broke it. "I wouldn't plan on being there Monday."

His voice was so hard, his tone so ruthless that a shiver raced through her. Rachel pushed back her chair and rose. "Thank you for your hospitality, but it's time I left. Michael and I will be leaving this morning."

She started for the door, and he let her get halfway across the room before he stopped her. "You won't get far without your passports, *cara*."

She froze, stiffening.

"I have the passports, yours and Michael's."

Slowly she turned to face him. "Did you go through my luggage?"

"They weren't in your hotel room. The hotel keeps them, remember? The front desk always takes your passport when you check in, and then returns it when you check out."

He was right. She'd forgotten all about her passport when she'd unpacked. She should have remembered before now. "You can't keep me here against my will. You assured me, promised me, that I was free to come and go." She was shocked that her voice managed to be so calm when her heart was thudding like mad. "But apparently your word means nothing. Apparently you have no integrity."

"Careful, *cara*," he said softly, rising from his chair to walk toward her. "Scandal is one thing. Slander is another."

Her eyes burned, hot and gritty. She drew a quick, furious breath, hands clenched at her sides. "But you did promise. You know you did."

"You are free to leave."

"You'll give me my passport?"

"I'll give you yours, yes. Of course. Do you want it?"

"Yes." Her chin notched up, eyes stinging from unshed tears. "I'll figure out another way. Michael and I don't need a lot. I'll leave my job and look for something else, a job where I can take him with me. Maybe I can be a nanny for another family and they'll let me bring Michael—"

He cut her off with a kiss, a hard, punishing kiss. Rachel's hands moved to his chest to push him away and yet she could feel his warmth through his cashmere sweater and her fingers curled into the softness, clinging to the material and him. She hated him and yet loved his smell and taste.

There was little tenderness in Gio's kiss. His lips parted hers, and he took her mouth with a fierceness that made her head spin. His tongue stroked the inside of her mouth, devastating her senses, sending rivulets of fire through her veins and creating an insistent ache low in her belly, an ache that made her thighs press, trying to stifle the need and how it coiled and curled within her, mocking her self-control.

She'd never felt longing until now.

She'd never wanted anyone as much as she wanted Giovanni.

She was breathless and dazed when he lifted his head. He stroked her flushed cheek, her skin so sensitive that his touch burned all the way through her, breasts tightening, nipples pebbling.

"You can go, *bella*, but my nephew stays," he said, lightly running his thumb over her swollen mouth, making it quiver beneath his touch. "You are an American. I have no claim over you. But Michael is, as you said, a Marcello, and he, as you said, belongs here, with his family."

His head dropped and his lips brushed hers and brushed again before he bit at her soft lower lip, sending a spark of pain through her, the pain immediately followed by pleasure. "But there is no need for you to go," he added. "There is no need for you to worry about anything. You can remain here as my wife and Michael's mother. It would solve many logistical problems, as well as protect the Marcello business and name."

Blinking back furious tears, Rachel gave him a hard shove. He didn't move. He didn't even sway on his feet. She yanked free instead, taking several steps back to put distance between them. "You can't do this," she choked. "You can't. I won't let you."

"And how will you stop me?"

"I'll go to the police—"

"You think they'll take your word over mine?"

"I'll go to the consulate. I'll ask for help."

"And you'll tell them what? That you came here with my nephew and summoned the media and attempted to blackmail me?"

"I never blackmailed you. I never threatened you in any way."

"No? Then you didn't summon the media? You didn't release a press statement?" He must have seen her surprise because he nodded. "I have a copy of the information you sent your media contacts. You have not behaved in an ethical manner. You will not look innocent or sympathetic to anyone."

"You can't take Michael from me!"

"I didn't take him. *You* abandoned him here."

"I never abandoned him!"

"You handed him to my servant and walked away. If I hadn't stopped you, you would have climbed in your water taxi and disappeared."

"You are turning this around. You are making me out to be someone I'm not. I only did what I did because I desperately needed help—"

"Obviously. And you're getting my help, because your desperation is jeopardizing a baby's welfare."

"No—"

"Yes. You knew nothing about me, or my staff, and your impulsiveness put Michael in danger."

Her chest squeezed tight, guilt mixing with fear. "I will not be manipulated."

"But *you* can manipulate *me*?" he retorted so softly that the hair rose on her nape and an adrenaline rush made her knees shake.

She couldn't speak. Her heart hammered double time. She stared at his chin and mouth to keep from looking into his eyes, afraid of what she'd see there. "Marriage is out of the question. You don't love me. You don't even like me. I refuse to sacrifice myself to further your business needs."

"But you'll sacrifice me, and my company, for your needs?"

"I haven't done anything. You are Machiavellian, not me."

"Because I am determined to protect my nephew, my company and my employees from a greedy American?"

She stepped forward, her hand lifting, and then she stopped abruptly, horrified that she'd come so close to slapping him. "You are twisting everything, poisoning my intentions. Fibs and lies and half-truths…" She drew a rough breath and then another. "Where does it end?"

"You came here to wage war, and you did, so don't expect sympathy from me, not when you were the aggressor."

"I was trying to help Michael!"

"If you marry me, then you have."

"Your business is not more important than my future."

"And Michael's?" he drawled quietly. When she didn't reply, he added, "You want Michael to be a Marcello, and you tell me that I need to do my part. But then, when I make an offer to you, you refuse it, saying you prefer to return to Seattle. *Cara*, I'm not sure you know what you want."

But that wasn't true. She knew what she wanted.

His money. His financial support so she could return to her life in Washington. She didn't want his money by becoming his wife! "You're not playing fair."

"You came here for financial support. I am offering you financial support." He studied her a moment, his lashes down, concealing his eyes, but then his lips curved in a slow heart-stopping smile. "Don't be foolish and proud, *bella*. Don't refuse what you so desperately need."

Rachel grabbed her coat and wallet from her room and left the palazzo, nearly running down the grand marble stairs and across the dramatic entry hall to exit through the house's front door.

She didn't care who saw her. She didn't care if the paparazzi were out with cameras fixed on the door, waiting the newest development in their scandalous story.

To hell with them. All of them, but especially Giovanni Marcello.

The afternoon was cold and the wind whipped the lagoon, sending the high tide sloshing over the canal bank onto the pavement. The sidewalk was wet but not nearly as flooded as yesterday. The tide must be coming down.

Rachel walked blindly down the Grand Canal for a block before turning at the corner and heading away from the busy street along a narrower canal. In her head she went through the last confrontation she'd had with Gio, pausing now and then to focus on something he'd said that was particularly infuriating.

Like the passport situation.

She'd forgotten all about the passports when she'd unpacked, but it wasn't that surprising as they hadn't been in her possession at the hotel, either. In the United States, the front desk did not retain the passports of international guests, but it seemed that it was the practice in Italy to collect them and keep them safe, and normally it wouldn't be a big deal, but she was outraged that the hotel would return them to Gio, and not her. And even more outraged that he had the audacity to keep them. Gio knew she wouldn't leave Italy without Michael. Gio knew he'd trapped her, and he wasn't at all remorseful. Rather, he was proud. *Pleased.* Giovanni the Conqueror. Giovanni the Villain.

She kicked hard at a deep puddle, sending water flying in every direction, drenching her legs. She shuddered at the cold, the damp chill doing nothing to improve her mood.

She wanted to leave Venice so badly. She hated being trapped and cornered. She hated that Giovanni had forced her to move into his home, and then he made it impossible for her to leave.

This visit to Venice had become a nightmare. She'd lost control the moment she rapped on the Marcello's front door. Why had she thought she could manage Giovanni? Why had she thought this could turn out any other way but unhappy?

Rachel didn't want to marry Giovanni. She didn't want a pretend engagement, much less a real one, never mind a wedding ring. She didn't want to live in Italy. But at the same time, she wasn't going to walk away from Michael.

What she wanted was to go home with Michael and hire a sitter and return to work and have some order in her life. She was tired of the chaos, tired of the stress, tired of things she didn't know and understand.

When Juliet got pregnant, it changed Rachel's life, too. Juliet wasn't the only one who became a mother, Rachel became the backup caregiver, and then after Juliet died, the surrogate mother. It hadn't been an easy transition for her. Rachael hadn't planned on becoming a mother for years. A decade or more. She'd planned on working until her midthirties at least, wanting to focus on career and the opportunity to save her money so that she'd have a proper nest egg, resources to sustain her in case of emergency, because God knew, life was full of emergencies. When one had spent one's life struggling and scrimping, budgeting and worrying, the idea of financial security was huge. Being financially independent would be life changing, and her plan was to do it for herself. She'd never dreamed that she'd wait for someone to take care of her. The idea of looking outward for support made her almost ill. No, she wanted to be strong and capable. She wanted to respect herself, and she would if she could provide for herself and any children she had.

Money, finances—those were such sensitive topics. Her mother certainly found it impossible to discuss financial topics with Rachel. She'd become emotional and cry, tearfully repeating that she was doing her best.

Rachel didn't want her mother crying or becoming defensive. She wasn't trying to criticize her mom; she just wanted to understand and help. How could she make things better for the family? How could she help ease some of the worry? It was a large burden. Mom was good at so many things, but managing money wasn't one of them.

Money, money, money…

Rachel wandered down streets until she approached St. Mark's Square. The famous piazza was lined with raised boards as the water was deeper here, flooding the entire square. She balled her hands inside her pockets and lowered her head to watch her steps.

How was she going to do this? How was she going to protect Michael and placate Giovanni? Because she wasn't about to marry a man she didn't love, and she most definitely wouldn't marry a man who didn't love her.

Rachel was many things—loyal, hardworking, determined—and those traits were evident. But she had a secret few people knew. She was privately, secretly terribly romantic.

She wanted love, big passionate love. She wanted the happy-ever-after and the lovemaking that resulted in fireworks and maybe even a few tears of joy.

She'd held out all these years for someone special, someone extraordinary. And she was determined to continue to hold out for the right one.

And the right one meant love, not lust. A small part of her—maybe a big part of her—desired Giovanni Marcello, but desire wasn't the answer and she was ashamed that she responded to him so easily. From now on, she would keep her distance. She had to. Otherwise Giovanni would have her in his bed, taking her virginity and the last shred of her self-respect.

Giovanni saw Rachel leave. He'd been at the window when she left the house, walking down the front of the Grand Canal to turn the corner and continue down the block. She disappeared for a few moments, and then reappeared as she cut down a narrow street.

She walked with her head bent and her hands buried deep inside her coat pockets until she entered an arched tunnel. If she kept going along that street, she'd eventually arrive close to St. Mark's square.

He wondered if that was where she was going.

He stood another moment looking out at the window before going to change into knee-high waterproof boots and his heavy winter coat.

He didn't know why he was going after her. She'd eventually return. She had no choice but to return, and he knew she'd never leave Michael. He'd seen her with the infant and she was as attached as a mother. She'd taken the little boy into her heart and was determined to provide the best possible life for him. He knew all that, and he didn't question her intentions, not anymore.

He didn't question her values, either. He understood what she wanted and it was the same thing he wanted for Antonio's son. But Michael couldn't have the life he needed, not if he was being juggled between Seattle and Venice, torn between countries and cultures, languages and customs, and Gio wouldn't lose Michael now that he was home.

Gio couldn't look at the infant without thinking of Antonio, and even though it hurt to remember Antonio, it was better than the emptiness of the past year. Gio had grieved for his brother for months, his death overshadowing everything. His brother had been his best friend from the time they were toddlers until they graduated from university as young men.

For the past six months Gio had done his best to avoid Michael. He hadn't wanted to meet this nephew of his, unable to tolerate more anger and more grief. And Gio was still angry, blisteringly angry that his brother decided not to try any of the experimental treatments that might have prolonged his life. He'd also been angry that Antonio spent so much of his last year alive in America instead of being home with his family, angry that his brother failed to take proper precautions and ended up conceiving a child with a shallow, self-serving woman who cared for no one and nothing but herself.

Antonio hadn't just thrown the rest of his life away. He'd crushed it and smashed it into the trash bin. It baffled Gio. Antonio had been among the smartest and the brightest, and he'd been a light in the world. He'd lit up a room with his keen wit and quick mind. He had a razor-sharp intelligence that he never used against another, not because he couldn't, but because he chose to build others up, to encourage them to be better.

Antonio had made Giovanni want to be better. Giovanni might have been the elder brother, but Antonio was his hero. Not because he was perfect, but because he genuinely tried to be good. To make a difference.

Gio's chest ached with bottled air. His hands fisted. Giovanni had lost Antonio but as long as he had Michael under his roof, his nephew was safe.

The high tides had kept all but the most curious and determined tourists out of the flooded neighborhoods, and the streets were mostly empty.

Normally Gio liked this Venice, when the streets were wet and he had entire blocks to himself, but today he could take little pleasure in anything until his personal life was settled. He wanted out of the press, out of the tabloid's headlines. It was bad for his corporation to have his personal life become news, particularly when it was featured on the gossip page instead of the business section.

It didn't take much to make investors jittery. It didn't take much to shake the confidence of world markets. He needed to protect the company, and he needed to protect his nephew. That was his focus and his chief concern. Everything else was secondary.

The water grew deeper as he approached Piazza San Marco. His boots sloshed through ankle-deep water as he entered La Piazza, Venice's most famous square, and the only one in Venice called *piazza*. He stepped onto the raised boards that skirted the square, elevating visitors and locals above the flooded area.

It struck him as he eased past a family grouped on the walkway that this was the first time he could remember chasing after anyone since he'd broken off his engagement. He hadn't cared enough about any woman to chase her. It's why he'd taken mistresses. It was a purely sexual relationship, a relationship he controlled, beginning and ending with gifts, leaving his emotions untouched.

He hadn't thought he'd ever feel again but the arrival of Michael unsettled him, and Rachel was waking him up, making him feel. He wasn't comfortable feeling anything. But he didn't seem to have a choice at the moment.

Gio followed the route he was certain Rachel had taken, splashing through water and then following the elevated boards as he approached St. Mark's Square.

Most of the shops and cafés surrounding the square were closed, but a few had remained open, with intrepid storekeepers placing wooden boards across the bottom of their open doors, keeping the water out while allowing customers in.

Gio checked in each open shop and café for Rachel. She wasn't in any of the bigger ones on the piazza, and he exited the square and turned a corner, spotting the small narrow coffee shop preferred by locals who'd stand and drink their espresso, and then leave, not requiring one of the three small tables at the rear.

Opening the door of the café, he stepped inside. There were just a few people at the counter. Beyond the counter were the tables, and two were empty, but at a third sat Rachel. She had a small cup in front of her but she wasn't drinking. Her hands were in her lap and her gaze was fixed on an unknown point in the distance.

She looked troubled. Lost. Gio's chest tightened. He drew a quick breath, surprised by the pang.

He nodded to the staff as he passed and drew out one of the empty chairs at Rachel's table. She looked up at him, the expression in her wide dark eyes a combination of sadness and despair, before her expression firmed, hiding her emotions. "What are you doing here?"

"Hunting you down."

"Why? I don't have a passport. I can't go anywhere."

"I was worried about you."

She exhaled softly, and he could see the sadness again, fear and vulnerability shadowing her eyes.

It made him uncomfortable, seeing her so fragile. His mistresses were strong and confident and needed nothing from him but sex and gifts. They didn't require excessive attention, never mind tenderness or protection.

"I'm tougher than I look," she said, chin jutting up, but there were tears in her eyes and she looked anything but tough.

Gio struggled with himself. He had been rough on her. He'd frightened her. He took little pleasure in wounding people. Much less women. But he also wasn't afraid of doing what needed to be done. Marrying Rachel would keep Michael in Venice. It was a contract, much like his arrangements with his mistresses. He wasn't doing it out of emotion, but practicality.

Yes, there were other ways to keep Michael in Venice. He could sue for custody. But legal cases of this nature took years, and he didn't want to spend years battling for custody when he could secure it quickly through marriage.

"I do not doubt that," he answered.

"I'm not afraid to fight you," she added.

"Obviously." He waited a moment. "But you won't win."

She searched his eyes, and he let her look, not hiding anything from her, because she needed to see who he was, she needed to understand what he was. Tough, driven, uncompromising. He did what he had to do. Always. And it's why he'd succeeded, because he always did what he had to do, even if it was painful.

"I keep trying to decide if you were teasing or bluffing," she said unsteadily.

"I don't bluff."

She looked hard into his eyes again, and then away. She sat across from him, cradling her cup, expression miserable, and the tension in his chest returned.

Despite the tension, he didn't try to fill the silence. He had learned early in his career to become comfortable with discomfort. He wasn't Antonio; his job wasn't to encourage or inspire. Gio's job was to make money and grow the company and take care of the Marcello employees, and that's what he did. Day in, and day out. Feelings didn't matter. Results mattered. Success. Stability. Financial accountability.

But it was hard to enjoy his single-minded focus when he sat across from a woman like Rachel. She wasn't Adelisa. He wasn't even sure what that meant, only she wasn't his ex-fiancée.

Rachel looked shattered all over again. "You know it's impossible."

"That, *cara*, is an exaggeration. It's not impossible. It's just…difficult."

"I don't want to marry you."

"And that is the difficult part."

CHAPTER TEN

HE WAS CRUEL beyond measure. Rachel's throat ached and her eyes burned. "I am nothing to you," she said quietly. "I am as insignificant as a bug, or a twig on the ground. You have no problem stepping on me, crushing me."

"That is not true."

"But my life and my dreams, they do not matter, not when you compare my needs to yours."

"I am responsible for a huge corporation. My decisions impact hundreds of people, if not thousands."

"You believe what you're saying, don't you? You're a demigod in love with your power." She hoped he heard the scorn in her voice. She hoped he was offended, because she was disgusted and appalled. There was nothing about him she admired.

"You are so consumed with your business. It seems to be the only thing that matters to you."

He leaned forward, narrowing the distance between them. "I have never put business before people. The various Marcello enterprises are made

up of people, and not just my family, but hundreds
of people, hundreds of loyal employees, and those
people matter to me a great deal. The best busi-
nesses treat their employees like partners...fam-
ily. Or, if you come from a seriously dysfunctional
family, then hopefully you treat your staff better
than family."

He'd inherited his family's business at a point
when the company family seemed irreparably
broken. The company was losing money, and his
father had decided that he'd rather live with his
mistress than his wife. Antonio was in America,
working for a business that was not their own, determined to get as far from their father as possible.

Gio envied Antonio, because Gio couldn't escape, not as the eldest, and he was surrounded by
the family drama, ensnared in it as Father's mistress was none other than his secretary, and the
affair had been going on for years, with Father and
secretary enjoying numerous "business" getaways
and long private lunches behind locked doors.

Italians loved a good drama, especially when
it was about sex and a beautiful young woman, a
woman young enough to be Giovanni Marcello
Senior's daughter.

Gio knew but couldn't convince his father to
fire the secretary or end the relationship, nor
would his mother divorce his father. Every day
was grueling and Gio tried to focus on work, not
wanting to be pulled into the middle of the family

drama more than necessary. Gio, like his grand-father before him, had a sharp mind and a love for engineering and practical design. He disliked the endless conflict that had marked his child-hood and adolescent years, and the only reason he'd agreed to work for Marcello Enterprises was because he loved the construction company his grandfather had founded.

But now, suddenly, the construction company, the Marcello holding company and even the fam-ily itself, was teetering on collapse. Gio was livid. He'd had enough, and he put his foot down. Either his father left, or he'd leave. That was all.

His father thought it was a joke, but Gio was furious that the company was being drained dry for selfish purposes when there were hundreds of employees that depended on the Marcellos. He'd never forget that last big battle with his father.

We owe our employees a solvent company. They shouldn't have to worry if they will have a job tomorrow, or a way to pay their bills. If you don't care about the future of a company that has been around for over one hundred years, get out now before you ruin the Marcello name.

And to Gio's surprise, his father left, abandon-ing ship, leaving his oldest son to save what he could.

That huge fight had been over fifteen years ago, and Giovanni had headed up the construction di-vision and the holding company ever since. It had been a massive struggle to turn the floundering corporation around, but he had. And so, yes, he was protective of the business, and even more protective of those who worked for him.

"The company is not one thing," he said. "It's not a bank account. It's not an office building. It's not equipment or real estate. It's people, *my* people. And I'm determined to do what is best for them. You see, they all have a vested interest in Marcello's success because each employee is gifted stock each year on the anniversary of their hire date. The longer an employee is with the company, the more stock they hold, which also means they become deeply invested in the company's success. When Borgo Marcello goes public in two weeks, my employees will have the opportunity to make some very good money. We've never done this before. Until now, all our companies have been privately held, but by going public, a number of my employees should make some good money. And that's what I want for them. This isn't about me. It's about rewarding those who have been loyal, when even my own family was not."

She exhaled slowly, staring out past Giovanni to the narrow street.

She didn't know what to say. She didn't know what to do with the information he'd just told her. In some ways she was relieved. But she was also more worried, because if what he said was true, he had very valid reasons for being so protective and proactive about his company.

She didn't want his employees to lose out on an exceptional opportunity. She'd never been offered stock at AeroDynamics, but Rachel did have friends who worked at high-tech companies and owning stock was huge, especially if a company was close to going public.

"There has to be some middle ground, though," she said after a moment. "Something that could protect your company and employees, and also protect me."

He looked at her and waited.

She swallowed hard. "Why does it have to be a real engagement, and a real marriage? Can't we just pretend until your company has gone public?"

"Pretend to be engaged…for an entire year?"

"A year? Why so long?"

"The first year a company goes public is quite volatile. I have no desire to add risk, or damage credibility." He paused, drummed his fingers on the table. "And Michael? What about him? A year from now he'll be eighteen months and walking and starting to talk. Will we want to tear his world apart right when he's becoming confident and secure?"

"He wouldn't know. He won't understand."

"He would if you suddenly left Venice."

Her eyes opened wide. "You expect me to live in Venice for the next year?"

"I expect you to live with me for the rest of your life."

Her lips parted in a silent gasp. Her stomach cramped. He was out of his mind, or far too sure of his power. Seconds passed, and then minutes. Rachel could not bring herself to speak, and Giovanni didn't seem interested in filling the silence, increasing the tension until she wanted to jump up and run. But where could she go? Nowhere. Because Michael was at the Marcello palazzo and she'd never leave Venice without him.

"You want to protect your company," she said carefully after an endless stretch of silence. "And I want to protect Michael. Surely we can both agree on that."

Gio's dark head inclined.

"I understand damage control is needed, especially since the media is fascinated with this fantasy story of ours, but eventually the media will move on to other stories and other scandals, and we can return to our lives, hopefully relatively unscathed."

Gio just waited.

She swallowed and mentally went through her thoughts before speaking them aloud, testing their strength and clarity. "Let's start with the pretend engagement. We can do that. It's not beyond our ability to smile in public and try to behave in a unified manner. It's a role we can manage for a few weeks, or even a few months. But let me be clear, I can't commit to anything longer than that. It's enough for us to take this first step now, implementing damage control, which should prevent the situation from spiraling."

He studied her from across the table, his gaze slowly examining every inch of her face. "So you'll stay here for the duration of the engagement?"

"I have a job, Gio, and I might not be the owner of my company but I have colleagues who count on me, and customers impatiently waiting my return—"

"I don't want you to return to Seattle, not if you're going to take Michael."

"Why not?"

"I don't want him with a stranger all day while you work. You deprive him of you. You deprive him of me. It's not right, not when I'm here, and I want him in my life."

"And what would I do if I stayed here?"

"Be his mother. Be my wife."

"And you'll compensate me, correct? You'll give me an allowance or open a bank account for me." She shuddered. "That is not my idea of a life. There is no independence. There is no freedom."

"Do you have freedom now? Show me your independence. You were on my doorstep begging for help."

Her lips compressed. She averted her head, her hands knotted in her lap.

"I know about your life in Seattle. You had a job, and a two-bedroom apartment—two bedrooms because Juliet often needed a place to crash—and a car with one more year of payments left on it. It's a life, a respectable life," he added quietly, "but it's not fantastic. It's not a dream. There's no reason you can't consider other options, and you need to consider other options, if not for your sake, then for Michael's."

She was so close to crying that she had to bite the inside of her lip hard, brutally hard, to keep the tears from falling. A marriage without love? What kind of future was that?

As if able to read her mind, he added, "Romantic love isn't everything. There is companionship. And passion. I will ensure you're satisfied—"

"Can you please drop this?" she choked, mortified.

"For now."

Leaving the café, they walked in silence for several minutes, pausing to let a group of tourists push past. They were talking loudly and in a hurry, and Rachel stepped back close to the building, glad for the interruption as it had been almost too quiet for the past few minutes.

Another group appeared on the heels of the first, and Rachel pressed her back to the building, letting the next group get by them, too.

"The water is receding," Gio explained. "The

tourists have been waiting anxiously in their hotels for the tides to drop, and now that high tide has passed, the tourists are descending on the city again.

"Does it flood this much every winter?" she asked as they started walking once more.

"We usually have a little bit of flooding every winter, but the amount varies. *Acqua alta*, which means high water, can range from just a few centimeters to three or four feet. Last year was a bad year. We had over four feet, and over half the island was covered. It was one of the worst seasons we've had in one hundred and fifty years."

"You sound so pragmatic."

"It can't be stopped, and Venice is never totally submerged. Even when it's bad, half the island is dry, and where we are now is the lowest part of the island. The piazza gets the worst of the high water, creating dramatic photos for tourists, but it doesn't bother residents. We expect *acqua alta*. Venice is an island, crisscrossed with canals. Water is part of our life. We can't escape it, nor would we want to."

"It's true, though, that the flooding has been worse in recent years, and that's due to climate change?"

"Venice has been sinking for hundreds of years, but it's not just because of climate change and the rising seas. The more we develop outlying areas, with the pumping of water and natural gas, the more Venice is negatively impacted. It is serious. It's devastating for those of us who love Venice."

She chewed on her lip, as she looked past him to the wet street beyond. "I think everyone loves Venice," she said after a moment. "How can you not? It's otherworldly. A fairy-tale city."

"So you could be happy here."

She shot him a pensive side glance. "I didn't say that."

"Then I will. You *could* be happy here. It's a fairy-tale city, a place where dreams come true."

Worn out from the emotional day, Rachel had dinner in her room, wanting some quiet and the chance to unwind with Michael.

She held him until after he'd fallen asleep in her arms and continued to hold him for another hour. She loved him so very much. The world was unpredictable and life could be overwhelming, but she was determined to protect him and do what was best for him until he no longer needed her.

He woke in the middle of the night, needing her. She walked him around his green room, and then around her room, making huge loops.

She kept the lights low and tried her best not to engage him, but at the same time she wasn't going to let him cry as he had last night. She didn't want a repeat of last night, where Giovanni was up and worrying about Michael, too.

As she paced, she glanced at the huge oil canvases on the wall, the green silk curtains with the thick gold and green fringe, the high ceiling and the gilt trim. Everything here was so old and valuable, centuries of wealth, and it boggled her mind just how different her world was, and how simple her needs really were.

She didn't need a lot. She didn't want a lot. Comfort was relative.

For Rachel, a comfortable life meant that she didn't have to worry about losing her home, or defaulting on car payments. A comfortable life meant that she could see a specialist when a second opinion was needed, or have a dinner out every now and then. Comfortable meant she could take a vacation once a year, renting a little beach cottage on the Oregon coast, something they'd all done in her family each summer when Dad was alive. She'd loved those annual trips to Cannon Beach and the lazy days where they did nothing but play cards and Scrabble and walk down the long sandy beach.

That had been her ideal life, the one she wanted for her children, when she had children. And now she had a child. She had Michael. She'd become a mother much earlier than she'd expected, and it'd been a shock, losing Juliet and discovering overnight that she was a single mom.

It had been beyond overwhelming. She'd never told anyone, but she'd been angry, too. She'd wanted so badly to have someone to confide in, but she'd worried that women would judge her, saying she was selfish, or lacking. But being a parent was such a huge responsibility and Rachel had wanted to do it right when she did become a mom. She'd wanted to have everything ready, in order. She'd wanted to be mentally prepared, and in a position to be able to be self-sufficient, or as self-sufficient as possible.

Not being able to tell anyone that she was scared and worried and also, yes, a little bit angry—or very much angry—had been isolating. It had left her even more alone because she had all these feelings that weren't socially acceptable, all these feelings where people would judge her for not being a real woman. For not being a good woman.

Rachel's eyes burned and stung. She blinked hard, trying to clear her vision.

All her life she'd struggled with the sense of inadequacy. She knew she was smart, capable, but it didn't seem to be enough. People valued beauty. So many in society placed beauty as the ultimate achievement. And beautiful was the one thing she'd never be, despite her attempts to improve her appearance through makeup and exercise and good hair care.

Throughout junior high and high school she'd pored over teen magazines with their tips on how to bring out one's natural beauty: lip pencil, eyeliner, contour and mascara. She did her face and hair every morning while in college, and continued with the full face routine every morning before work, but the makeup was a mask. It merely served to hide how plain she was beneath, and how fragile her confidence really was.

That was something else no one knew.

She looked polished and professional on the outside, but on the inside, she was filled with self-doubt, and those self-doubts and recriminations had only grown since Juliet died. Like the city of Venice during *acqua alta*, Rachel was drowning.

Gio was surprised to see Rachel appear in the doorway of the breakfast room at a relatively early hour. She was already dressed, wearing charcoal trousers and an oversize sweater, and didn't seem to be wearing any makeup. Her hair had been drawn back into a ponytail high on her head, with just a few shorter wisps loose to frame her face.

She looked pretty, but tired, with lavender shadows beneath her brown eyes.

"Good morning," she said. "I was told this is where breakfast is being served today."

"Yes," he answered, rising and drawing a chair out for her. "Join me."

She sat down, thanking him in a low voice. With her now seated at his side, he could feel her exhaustion.

"Michael had you up again last night, didn't he?" Gio asked.

"It's all right. I'm used to it."

"I don't think it's good for you. I'd like a night nurse to take over in the evenings, at least for the next few weeks. You need your rest, too. It's hard to keep a level head when you're short on sleep, and we have a lot going on right now."

Her brow creased, expression troubled. "So you intend to announce our engagement when?"

Before he could answer, the door opened and the maid appeared. Gio looked at Rachel. "Would you like American coffee or an espresso?"

"Do you have coffee by the pot? I feel like I need gallons of it today."

Gio gave the instructions to his maid and then waited for her to leave. "It's been done," he said as the door closed. "I had my PR firm release the information last night."

Her jaw dropped, horrified. *"What?"*

Gio reached for the stack of folded papers on the seat of the empty chair next to him. He'd read them earlier and saved them to show her. He placed the papers in front of her, with the English version on top to make it easier for her, watching her expression as she scanned the paper's bold headline.

Italian Billionaire Marcello to Marry American Lover!

"You really did tell them," she whispered.
"I needed to. Media outlets from all over the

world have been calling my company, and the company has been trying to send everyone to the PR agency, but it's out of control right now."

She lifted the paper, unfolding it to see the accompanying photo. It was a new one, taken of them yesterday in the coffee shop off the piazza.

For a long moment she said nothing, and then she sighed, the sound that of disappointment and perhaps resignation. "Are they all like this?" she asked, shuffling through the papers to glance at each.

"Yes."

She flipped through the papers again. "How long will this...attention...last?"

"As long as we remain newsworthy."

"I'd like to end the newsworthy element as soon as possible."

"I could not agree more. It's why we're going to push forward quickly, and do a news dump, releasing all the announcements and information at one time so there are no more surprises and no more big headlines."

"How does that work?"

"We're sending out the invitations for our engagement party today. Once they are in the mail, we'll make an announcement about the party and perhaps do an exclusive interview with one of the bigger tabloids, inviting them into the palazzo and letting them have a look at the party preparations, or even better, plans for our wedding."

"But you're so private. Won't that just whet the paparazzi's appetite for more?"

"I think once I'm more accessible, they'll grow bored."

"You hope," she said.

"I do."

She looked up at him, her eyes bright, her cheeks pink, her emotions right there on the surface. He liked her transparency. He liked that she wasn't the schemer he'd first thought. She was nothing like the kind of women he spent time with, and maybe that was why he was drawn to her. She was fresh and real and emotionally accessible. Her emotions made her more beautiful: the light that shone in her eyes, the quick curve of her lips, the vexed expression when provoked.

She was provoked now. "You expect me to capitulate, don't you? You're expecting me to just acquiesce and marry you."

"Yes."

"You will be disappointed."

"I don't think so. I think you will soon discover that love is overrated, especially when the sex is deeply satisfying."

She flushed and her jaw firmed.

"Or perhaps you've never enjoyed sex—"

"That's enough," she choked. "Nothing about this conversation is appropriate."

"How are we to make love if we can't even discuss it?"

"We're not going to make love, or get married. I have agreed to a pretend engagement. That is all."

She was so flustered, her cheeks were dark pink, her voice breathless. He didn't think she was faking it, either. Rachel was a different species of woman, and it made him wonder, if she was this emotional and sensitive at the breakfast table, what would she be like in his bed?

The thought made him hard, and a little impatient. He pushed the papers back toward her. "Then what do we do? Have photographers chase you every day? Lie in wait for you and Michael as you run errands? The life you once had is gone, Rachel. This is your life now."

She said nothing, her chin jutting in displeasure.

He could change that expression with a kiss. He was tempted, too, but first, he needed to explain something. She needed to understand his concerns.

Gio searched through the papers until he found the one that had reprinted the photo of her carrying Michael to the doors of the palazzo. The photographer had zoomed in on the baby, taken a close-up of him wrapped in the blanket. The headline was simple. It read, The Billionaire's Baby, but it was enough.

The one photo, coupled with the three words, summed up the dangerous situation Rachel had unwittingly created. Michael was a story, a fascinating story, and people wanted a piece of it. Of him.

Gio placed the Italian paper on top of the English one. He tapped the photo as he read the headline to her, translating it from Italian to English. She looked at him, dark arching brows drawn.

"My grandfather Marcello had an older brother," Gio told her quietly. "He was kidnapped during an outing, taken right from the arms of his mother during a morning walk. The kidnappers demanded a million dollars. My great-grandparents paid the ransom. Their fourteen-month-old was returned to them, in a box."

"Dead?" she whispered.

He nodded. "It was a sensational story, and the three men were eventually arrested, tried and found guilty. But it didn't bring back the child. My grandfather grew up aware that he was the replacement, and equally aware that his birth did nothing to assuage his mother's grief. Money does not always solve problems. Wealth can make one a target. I do not want Michael vulnerable, and yet you, *cara*, have made him so."

Gio could see the effect of his words. Rachel paled and grew still. He almost regretted putting the blame on her shoulders, but she had to understand, the world he inhabited was not like hers. His world was one of power and prestige, but also envy and greed. People could be dangerous. Gio had to protect Michael—and Rachel—from those that would try to destroy them.

The breakfast room was unbearably quiet.

Heartsick, Rachel felt hot and then cold, her stomach plummeting. Last night as she'd paced with the baby, she'd thought about money, and how important it was for her to feel stable and secure. She'd never considered the flip side, and how having a great deal of money could become a trap. "I'm sorry," she said, meaning it. "I'm sorry to have brought Michael to the world's attention. It makes me sick—"

"We just need to be careful from now on. We need to make sure he has the right people around him and be sure he's not exposed to danger."

She nodded jerkily, eyes gritty, trying to wrap her head around Michael's future. He would forever be an heir now: the boy who'd inherit a fortune. It wasn't the life she'd wanted for him. She hadn't wanted to change his life, just improve it. "I wish I could go back... I wish I'd known."

"What's done is done. Now we need to make the best of it."

"But won't a party here invite trouble into your home?"

"I have already vetted the guest list, and there will be security, a great deal of it."

She said nothing and he pressed on.

"The party will be on Saturday, next week. We'll host the event in the grand ballroom. With the invitations going out in today's mail, it will keep the ball from looking like a rushed affair."

"A *ball*? Not a cocktail party? Something simple?"

"It's impossible to host anything in a seventeenth-century ballroom without it looking like a major event. Besides, everyone likes to dance."

"But I don't see how an engagement *ball* will solve any of our problems!"

"It will add legitimacy to our relationship, publicly solidifying us as a couple. People will enjoy helping us celebrate our commitment to each other and Michael."

"Speaking of Michael, when will we tell everyone that Michael is actually Juliet and Antonio's?"

"Never."

"*What?* Why not?"

"There is no need to make an announcement. Those close to us will know the truth. But the rest, why correct them? It's no one's business but ours—" He broke off as Anna returned with coffee and breakfast.

Rachel murmured thanks for her coffee but couldn't even look at the food, far too shaken by the developments. "How many people are you inviting to this party?"

"Two hundred and sixty. I anticipate we will have about two hundred actually attend."

"That's a huge party."

"The ballroom is huge."

"Then put the party in another room, your mother's favorite room, for example. We could have twenty in there and it would be lovely."

"That sounds lovely and intimate, but it won't communicate what we want it to. A large, lavish party doesn't just convey confidence, but excitement, and joy…all the things we want the public to associate with our marriage."

"Our engagement, you mean. A faux engagement, at that."

He shrugged. "The goal is to present a united front to all. Even to those in our inner circle."

"What about your mother?"

"I will tell her what she needs to know."

"The *truth*."

"I am not going to create worry and anxiety for her, not if I don't have to."

"I am not an actress, Gio. I am not good at pretending. I can't even lie well. I don't know why, but if I tell a fib, I immediately blush—"

"That is why you will marry me. Then you won't have to worry that about your acting skills. You won't have to act, or lie. There would be no faux engagement, just a real one, ending in a real wedding. Michael will have his family. You will be able to focus on the baby. I can focus on my business. Everything will be as it should be."

CHAPTER ELEVEN

EVERYTHING WOULD BE as it should—for him.

He would have an heir for his business. He'd have a mother for his nephew. He'd have a warm body for his bed. It was all so easy and convenient for him. She'd made it so easy and convenient.

She inhaled, and then exhaled, face hot, chest on fire. "You don't even regret having a marriage of convenience, do you?"

"I don't romanticize marriage anymore, no."

"But you once did?"

He shrugged. "Once upon a time I was naive."

"What happened?"

"We got engaged, we nearly married, but in the nick of time I discovered she didn't want me. She simply wanted a rich husband."

Rachel went cold, suddenly understanding just why he loathed Juliet so much, and why he'd been so mistrustful of her, too. "I don't want a rich husband," she whispered. "I don't want a husband at all—"

"I understand. But there are consequences in life. We both know that, and we both know marriage would be the best thing for a child that has lost both mother and father before he's even seen his first birthday."

"Everything is suddenly *we* and *us*, but three days ago you wouldn't even say his name!"

"Three days ago I had an attorney working on custody." Giovanni's gaze met hers. "I was preparing to take him from you. And then you showed up on my doorstep with him…and left him. You played right into my hands."

"I don't believe it. You're just saying that. You've never acknowledged him. You've refused to acknowledge him."

"I have spent these past few months researching the legitimacy of your claim, and then considering my options, including suing for sole custody, cutting you out completely. Before I could decide what was the best course of action, you appeared here, forcing my hand." He studied her from across the table. "Suing for custody might still be the best option. That is, if we don't choose to raise him together."

"As a married couple."

He nodded.

She laughed shortly. Why was she not surprised? "You do not play fair."

"Life isn't fair. But I am doing my best to make it as fair as possible for our nephew, whom I believe you care for."

"I love him dearly."

"Then it cannot be such a huge sacrifice to stay here and raise him with me."

She held her breath, heart pounding.

He filled the silence. "You strike me as an extremely capable woman. I have full confidence in you, and that you'll be able to adjust to your new life. Otherwise, I wouldn't marry you. I'm marrying you, I'm making you my wife, a Marcello, because you have the qualities I admire in a woman, and the qualities that would make a good wife and an excellent mother."

"And it doesn't bother you that I don't love you?"

"It would bother me more if you said you did."

Her stomach lurched. "That's horrendous."

"I don't trust romantic love. It's false and changing."

"And I think a loveless marriage is horrific. It makes marriage sound lonely and cold."

"I promise you our marriage won't be cold, not if we're sharing the same bed."

"Sex isn't the answer to everything!"

"Then you haven't had the right partner. Great sex is deeply satisfying."

She couldn't stop blushing. "You are overly confident."

He looked at her for an endless moment, before smiling faintly, looking every bit the confident, arrogant man she'd met her first day here. And when was that? Just two days ago? God, it seemed like a lifetime. Everything was changing, the tides were rising, flooding her world, and she couldn't seem to save herself. "I'll make you a deal then. You come up with a plan that is better. A plan that immediately protects Michael and gives him a family, as well as financial security. Then tell me and we will do that. But if you can't propose anything better, we will marry and move forward with our lives."

He glanced at his watch and grimaced. "I hate to leave on that note, but I have a conference call in a few minutes, and it's one that I can't miss." He pushed back from the table and started from the room, but then stopped before he reached the door. "This is not an easy situation, not for either of us, and I'm sorry."

And then he was gone.

After the conference call finally ended an hour later, Gio remained at his desk, deep in thought. It had been a difficult call, not because of the subject matter, but because he'd found it almost impossible to focus.

Rachel had said she didn't want a cold, passionless, loveless marriage. He agreed with her on that point, but he wasn't worried that they'd have a cold relationship, or passionless, not when he wanted her as much as he did.

He'd been attracted to her from the start, and he'd fought the attraction, just as he'd tried to ignore how much he'd liked kissing her. He loved her mouth, the softness and the fullness, and how she couldn't quite help kissing him back. It made her sexy. Delicious. He wanted to kiss the rest of her. He wanted to strip her and explore those gorgeous curves—hips, breasts, thighs and in between.

In the beginning he hadn't understood why he was so drawn to her. She wasn't like the women he'd dated, and that was her appeal.

But he was tired of all the words. He wasn't a man of words. He was a man of action.

He'd take her to his bed. He'd show her that he could please her. He'd show her that she could be happy with him.

Gio left his desk and walked to the tall arched leaded glass windows that looked over the narrow lagoon. It was another gray day with wisps and tendrils of fog rising from the water. The fog was supposed to get heavier as the day ended, shrouding the streets and water in a cloak of mystery. He loved this Venice, and Rachel would grow to love it, too.

He'd woo her tonight. He'd delight her, pleasure her, and in his bed, she'd become his. There would be no more fighting or protesting. She'd discover she liked being in his bed, and she'd realize she'd liked being *his*.

Gio glanced out at the lagoon once more before returning to his desk. The fog made it the perfect night to go out. They would travel in the Marcello gondola, one of the most elegant boats in the city. It had the patina of age, being well over a hundred years old, and glamorous, the outside lacquered in gleaming black paint while the interior was upholstered in black leather and cream and opulent gold leaf.

He knew where he'd take her for dinner, too. Il Sussurro. It was his favorite restaurant on the island, and without a doubt, the most exclusive. It was incredibly difficult to get a reservation, not just because Il Sussurro had only four tables, but because it was booked out years in advance.

Fortunately, Gio did not have to pull any strings to secure a table, as there was always one waiting for him. Indeed, the fifth-floor table was his, just as the fifth floor was his, which wasn't saying much as the floors of the medieval building were quite narrow, the house built snug, like a ship, each floor consisting of a single room and the central hall with the circular staircase.

Fifteen years ago he helped finance Il Sussurro when no one else would give the chef and restaurateur a loan. The concept of Il Sussurro was like its name—a whisper, a murmur—small enough to be overlooked, maybe even forgotten.

No commercial lender was willing to risk the money on a restaurant that would not even be able to seat twenty-four people each evening. Where was the profit margin in that? While traditional banks questioned the viability of such a venue, Gio immediately grasped the appeal. Privacy. Novelty. Exclusivity.

Intrigued by the vision for the 1384 building, he'd funded the restoration and refurbishment, and Il Sussurro proved to be a huge success.

Gio made a call to Carlo, one of the owners of Il Sussurro, advising his old friend that he'd be dining at his table tonight.

"How many, Gio?" Carlo asked.

"Just two," Giovanni answered. "And it's a special occasion."

"It's always a special occasion when you join us."

"Grazie, Carlo. We'll see you later tonight."

Hanging up the phone, he called Allegra Paladin, the founder of Paladin, a Venice-based fashion house founded by a former mistress. When he ended the relationship five years ago he'd given her enough money that she'd been able to open her own business.

On the phone, he told Allegra about the dress he was looking for. It was a couture gown from her September show. The dress was floor-length with a formfitting bodice and long sleeves. There might have been a small collar, he wasn't sure, but the neckline was a deep V, and the color an olive green. Dusty rose flowers were embroidered on the green lace bodice, with larger, looser rose and gold roses scattered on the long sheer skirt.

"I know the one," Allegra answered, amusement in her voice. "But it's not your size, my darling."

"Mmm, funny, but I think you know it's not for me."

She sighed, the sound wistful. "It's true, then? You really are engaged?"

"You'll meet the right man one day, I promise."

"You were the right man."

"I wasn't."

"I should have gotten pregnant," she pouted.

"*Allegra*," he said, a warning in his tone.

"I'm not sure how she managed it. You were always so zealous about protection with me."

"I don't want to have this conversation. But I do want the dress. I need it today, and it will have to be shortened. Can you send a seamstress with it to the house this afternoon?"

Allegra hesitated. "She doesn't seem your type."

"But that's just it," he said quietly. "She *is* my type. She's exactly my type."

"Does that mean you've finally fallen in love, Gio?"

"I'm not sure Rachel would be comfortable with this conversation."

"You are in love," she said, wonder in her voice. "When is the wedding? Have you set the date?"

"We're keeping the details private for now, but it's soon. Very soon."

* * *

Rachel was playing with Michael after his afternoon nap when a knock sounded on her door. Opening her door, she discovered Anna in the hall with a middle-aged woman carrying an oversize red garment bag with silver script on it, reading *Paladin*.

"Signor Marcello..." Anna paused, frowning, as if uncertain how to explain.

But then Gio was there to take over. "Has something for you," he said, stepping around the women to enter Rachel's room as if it was his. He crossed to Rachel and took the baby from her, as if the baby was his, too. "The dress is for tonight," he added, holding Michael comfortably against his chest, the baby's diapered bottom resting on his arm. "I hope you'll like it."

Rachel watched as the older woman unzipped the bag and drew out a gleaming green gown, shot with gold threads with pops of rose and light gold flowers. "Oh, it's gorgeous."

"Do you like it?"

"I do. But why wear it tonight? Shouldn't I save it for the engagement party?"

"We're going out tonight. I've booked a reservation somewhere special."

"Won't people see us...or did you want that?"

"It's going to be foggy tonight, a perfect night for us to slip out and not be seen. We'll leave here at eight. Does that work for you?"

"Yes."

"Good. And now the seamstress from Paladin is going to hem the dress for you, and make any other adjustments necessary."

Rachel had never owned a dress like this one before. The bodice hugged her breasts and waist before spilling in a waterfall of silk and lace to her feet. The sheer lace sleeves made her skin gleam and she didn't think she'd ever felt so feminine before. She struggled with her hair, uncertain as to whether she should put it up or leave it down. In the end she drew it into a low side ponytail because she felt too bare wearing it up, and it was so heavy when she left it down.

Rachel was in the great hall right at eight, and yet Gio was already there, waiting for her. "Don't tell me I'm late again," she said, shifting her black wool coat to the other arm.

"No. You're right on time. But you're not going to wear that coat tonight, so give it to me."

"What will I wear instead?"

"A cape."

"Like Batman and Robin?" She laughed.

"Or like a princess from the eighteenth century." He lifted the black velvet cloak from the banister and draped it over her shoulders before loosely tying the braided silk ribbon at her throat to keep it from falling off her shoulders.

The brush of his fingers against her neck sent

a shiver of pleasure from her, while the long velvet, fur-lined cloak felt like heaven. It was soft and yet with enough weight to cocoon her in warmth.

"I didn't think I could possibly feel more elegant," she said breathlessly, "and yet I do."

"Wait. I'm not quite done. There is one more small adjustment to make," he said, drawing something from his trouser pocket. "These are not old. Nor are they family pieces. It's something I bought for you today." He opened the small bronze leather pouch and shook out a pair of earrings, the dark green stones spilling into his palm, glimmering with color and light. "I worried that the green might be a little off, but they're such quality stones that I thought it was worth it."

She was almost afraid to touch the earrings, each one made of two emeralds, a large oval at the lobe, with a huge teardrop emerald beneath. "They're real?" she whispered.

"Yes."

"They're so big."

"They are dramatic, but they'll suit you."

"I hope you're not spending money on me. I don't want you to—"

"Don't deprive me of the pleasure of treating you." He tilted her chin up and slipped the slim gold post through the hole in her earlobe before attaching the back, holding the decadent earring in place. "Now the other ear."

"This isn't a treat. It's called spoiling. The dress, the cape, the earrings."

"Hasn't anyone ever spoiled you before?"

"No."

"That's criminal. You deserve to be draped in jewels."

Rachel couldn't help laughing. "As if I were a courtesan in a Turkish harem?"

"Or a young bride, anticipating her wedding day."

She flushed, blood surging to her cheeks, making her face feel hot and sensitive. "Now you're making me nervous."

"No need to be nervous. Enjoy being spoiled."

She dipped her head to hide her blush. "Thank you for the gifts...for all of them."

"My pleasure. You look beautiful."

She glanced up, her smile unsteady. "I think, though, I know what you are doing."

"And what is that?"

"You're trying to break down my resistance. You want to win me over."

Deep grooves bracketed his mouth. His bright blue eyes glowed down at her. "I've already won you over. You just haven't admitted it yet." His head dropped, and his lips brushed hers, lightly, fleetingly, sending a sharp tingle up and down her spine. "But you will, soon."

The boat slid through the lagoon, the gondolier standing at the back, eyes sharp, seeing what they

couldn't, steering with hardly a splash. The night
was so quiet and still with the fog. The streetlamps
looked like distant balls of light. The stillness created a magic, and Rachel found herself holding
her breath again and again, senses heightened and
delighted.

They soundlessly slipped from one canal to another, turning corners she didn't even see, easing
under bridges that popped out of nowhere. She
was grateful the gondolier knew the city so well
because she was completely lost, and yet it felt
good to give up control. It was almost a relief.
She'd been fighting so hard to keep everything together and tonight she could control nothing—not
the dark, or the fog, or the direction they were to
go. She could only sit and feel, exquisitely aware
of Giovanni next to her, his tall, imposing frame
hard, his muscular body warm.

She couldn't see far. Sometimes she saw nothing, but there were other moments when she
could just make out the shape of a building, or
the shadow of a person walking on the pavement,
footsteps muffled by the fog. Every now and then
the gondolier's oar splashed, or they'd pass another gondola and the drivers would murmur a
greeting as the boats slid by.

It was all a fantasy, she thought, a seductive
dream that was lulling her, relaxing her so that she
found herself leaning against Gio, letting him support her weight. She could feel his thigh against

hers, and her shoulder against his chest. His arm was around her, his palm flat against her waist, his fingers just brushing her tummy, and it shouldn't be anything, but it was. It was intense. It all felt dizzying and overwhelming and she was feeling things she had never felt before, and imagining his hand on her bare skin, his fingers caressing her, stroking her, finding the curve of her breast and the hollow between her legs.

She wanted him to touch her and explore her—

"You're cold?" he said, his voice near her ear, feeling her shiver.

"Just a little," she lied, almost boneless with need, before drawing a tremulous breath. He'd been right earlier. She *was* starting to fall for him. She wanted him and was teased by the idea of a life with him. No one had ever taken care of her before. No one had ever spoiled her or desired her, either...

But desire wasn't love, and the risk was huge. She was falling for him; she could have her heart broken.

"We're nearly there." He held her tighter, closer, his fingers so very close to the apex of her thighs that she was stunned she hadn't burst into flames.

She didn't understand the attraction, or the emotions sweeping through her. She didn't understand how she could be falling for someone who was also such a threat. Maybe the problem was that she had never felt this kind of intense

physical attraction before. Maybe the problem was
that she had never felt this way about *anyone* before. Her feelings were not intellectual, nor were
they rational. Her feelings really weren't feelings
but hope and desire, fear and need. It began as a
baffling, carnal desire that had bypassed her head
to fill her body, humming in her veins, and had
turned into a curiosity and hunger that made her
want him to want her—not just her body, but her
mind, and her heart—all of her.

She turned her head and looked at his darkly
handsome profile and felt everything inside her
tighten and flip.

He was beautiful. There was no denying it. But
that wasn't a good thing, not in this instance, because honestly, he was too beautiful for her. And
he wasn't just ridiculously handsome, he was also
brilliant and successful. Wealthy beyond belief.
Women like her didn't get men like him. No, Gio
was the kind of man Juliet snagged, the kind of
man who wanted perfection on his arm. Even
dressed in an expensive gown and draped in velvet and fur and jewels, she wasn't perfection. She
wasn't even close.

He would not be happy being married to her. He
would resent her, and that would be intolerable…
It would break her heart.

Gio didn't know what happened, but something
did. One moment Rachel was happy and relaxed,

leaning into him, and then the next she'd become stiff, her slim shoulders hunched, head bowed.

"What's wrong?" he asked.

"Nothing," she answered.

"Something has upset you. You're sad."

She lifted her head but couldn't quite look him in the eyes. "This is a mistake, you know. All of this."

"The boat ride? The earrings? What?"

"The gifts, the date, the proposal." Her voice cracked. "The marriage. You would hate it, and I would hate it, and we'd be miserable, trapped together, and I can't do more misery. I've had enough misery and enough guilt to last a lifetime."

"What do you feel guilty about?"

"What *don't* I feel guilty about?" He saw her lift a hand to the gentle sway of her emerald earring. "And then you buy me these beautiful things as if I deserve them, but I don't. I am not who you think I am, and I am not someone you will be happy with. Please, just let me take Michael home. Please—"

He silenced her anguished words with a kiss, not to stifle her, but to try to comfort her. He kissed her deeply, melting her resistance, kissing her until she was no longer stiff and chilled, but warmly pliant, her body pressed to his.

Aware that they were no longer moving, he lifted his head. Her dark eyes still glittered with a hint of tears, but something else, too. "I don't know what you've done, or why you feel guilty, but I don't believe it's as bad as you think," he said quietly.

She struggled to smile but failed. "Your fiancée…why did you fall in love with her?"

"She was beautiful and glamorous and exciting."

"I'm none of those things."

"Thank God you are not shallow or superficial. We wouldn't be marrying if you were."

"Not even for Michael's sake?"

"No. I'd take him from you. I'd sue for custody and be done with you."

"Without a hint of remorse?"

"With absolutely none."

His candor surprised her. She blinked at him, her dark eyes wide, expression bemused, and then the confusion lifted and she laughed. "You sound like a dreadful man."

"I am." And then he kissed her lightly before releasing her. He rose and stepped from the gondola and extended his hand to her. "But if anyone can manage me, it's you."

She'd felt distraught just a few minutes ago and yet he'd somehow turned the moment around, dispelling the shadows, first with his kiss, and then with his words.

She didn't know how he did it, but she was grateful. Rachel gathered the billowing cape and put her hand into his, and stepped from the gondola onto the pavement. However, as she stepped out, her high heel caught in the hem of her long lace gown and she lurched forward, losing her balance.

Gio was there, though, his hands circling her waist, preventing her from falling.

He used the momentum to draw her against him and hold her there. She exhaled hard. One moment she was tumbling through space, and the next she was in his arms, pressed to his hard frame, feeling every bit of his sinewy strength.

She ought to pull away, and yet for the first time in ages she felt safe. She felt supported. She wasn't alone.

It crossed her mind that she didn't want or need the jewels and gowns, but she wanted *him*. She very much wanted him: heart, mind, body and soul, and she was ready to be seduced, ready to feel more, and have more, and be more. And so she stood there, letting his warmth penetrate her long black cloak, penetrate her tingling skin, piercing all the way to the marrow of her bones.

If he kissed her now, she'd kiss him back. If he kissed her now, she would reach out and clasp his nape, her fingers slipping into his dark crisp hair. She'd stand on tiptoe and savor the feel of his lips on hers. She'd taste him and explore his mouth the way he explored hers. She would take advantage of the opportunity to feel, wanting to feel every nuance possible.

His arm tightened around her waist, and his lips brushed her temple. "I'm afraid to let you go," he said. "The last thing I need is you falling into the lagoon."

His lips sent the most delicious shivery sensation through her and she couldn't quite hide her smile. "Don't worry," she murmured. "I can swim."

His lips brushed over her eyebrow. "Yes, but a gentleman wouldn't just stand there and watch a lady splash about. I'd have to come in after you and be heroic. It would be most annoying."

She laughed a low husky laugh. It was hard to think straight; her pulse was racing and her head felt light, making her giddy. "Indeed, because then we would both be cold and wet. Far better for me to be the only wet one."

"But of course once we reached the palazzo, I would have to be sure you were all right. I would have to send you to a hot bath, and then make sure you were towel dried properly, and then wrapped in a robe. I would insist you were seated before a fire with a glass of warm brandy in your hands, and that you stayed there until there was no chill left and you were warm inside and out. I would have to stay close and be sure you were following directions. It would require considerable time and energy on my part, and I am quite sure you would find my ministrations tedious."

"It does sound awful," she murmured unsteadily, leaning against him, her breasts pressed to his chest.

"It would be awful," he agreed, his head dropping, dipping, his mouth brushing the shell of her ear. She shuddered at the warmth of his breath and the way her nerves danced with awareness.

"See? You are shivering with distaste," he added, sliding a hand over her throat, slipping up to outline her chin and then the delicate bones of her jaw. "Imagine how unhappy you would be, locked in my room, naked before my fire."

She shivered again, with anticipation and nerves. "I think it's time to feed you dinner. You sound hungry, and a little bit barbaric."

"I am hungry, but it's you, *cara,* I want."

CHAPTER TWELVE

RACHEL HAD NEVER enjoyed a meal in a private dining room before, let alone served by their own waiter, with a crackling fire in a massive stone fireplace keeping them warm.

The food had been amazing, course after course, with far too much wine, and now that all the dishes had been cleared for coffee, she couldn't help sighing with pleasure. What an incredible restaurant, what a special meal. The company, though, was the best part. Giovanni Marcello had to be the ultimate dream date.

"I don't want you worrying anymore," Gio said, breaking the comfortable silence. "There is no reason for you to struggle and juggle and feel desperate about anything. I can provide for you, easily."

Rachel stared into his darkly handsome face. He wasn't the stranger he'd been when she arrived at the beginning of the week. She didn't know him well, but there was an undeniable attraction, as well as a connection between them, that hadn't been there days ago. "I'm afraid if I married you, I'd lose myself."

"I'm not going to own you, no more than you'd own me."

"I don't think anyone could ever own you. You are far too strong, too independent."

"You're every bit as strong as me."

She gave her head a small shake. "I'm not, though. If you really knew me, you wouldn't be impressed."

"Maybe it's time you explained. Why do you feel so guilty?"

She shook her head, not just unwilling to tell him, but unable. She knew the words would horrify him. They horrified her. "I can hardly admit the truth to myself. I can't imagine what you would think."

"Tell me." He reached across the table and stroked her cheek. "*Cara, bella*, I promise you it isn't as bad as you think."

She didn't agree, but she was tired of all the emotions bottled inside of her, and truthfully, she wanted him to know, especially since he was so determined to marry her. It might change his mind. "I didn't want to be a single mother. I didn't want to do it this way. I wanted to wait until I was ready and I could be a good mom, and I'm not… I'm not…and I hate myself for being like Juliet. Selfish and self-absorbed—" She bit ruthlessly into her lower lip to keep the words from spilling out. Because even now, she could feel how black the truth was, and how ugly it made her.

Rachel had deliberately set the bar high for herself. She'd done it because she was different from Juliet. Stronger. Smarter. *Better.*

"How are you like her?" he demanded. "What have you done that is so selfish and self-absorbed?"

"I've resented that I was needed to help manage Juliet's life…sorting her problems, fixing her mistakes. And then when Juliet fell in love with Antonio, and ended up pregnant, I was livid, because it's one thing to overdraw your checking account, but it's another to have a baby." She pushed at the lone spoon still on the tablecloth. Her eyes burned but she could not cry. "Juliet never had to stand on her own feet. She'd always had Mother, and then when Mother was gone, Juliet couldn't cope anymore, and she died, and I inherited her son."

Rachel let her lashes fall, and she held her breath, wondering when Gio would speak, wondering what he'd say, but he was silent.

After a moment she forced herself to continue. "I wasn't happy about how my life changed. I resented a three-month-old baby. I resented my own nephew…" She bit down into her bottom lip. "How could I do that to Michael? How could I hate him when he did nothing wrong?"

"You didn't hate him."

"No, but I wasn't happy. And when Juliet died, I didn't feel love. I just felt anger. And mostly anger with her because I felt like she took my choices away from me."

"Those are normal emotions," Gio said quietly. "Anyone would feel that way."

Rachel swallowed with difficulty. "I lived so much of my life in Juliet's shadow…and then once she was gone, I still lived in her shadow." Her head lifted and she looked at Gio. "Being a single mom was not my plan. It was really important to me that I could be self-sufficient and financially independent before I married and had children. Instead, look at me. I show up, begging on your doorstep."

"You weren't begging. You were fierce and very defiant."

She wished she could smile but couldn't. "I can't forgive myself for being angry with Juliet, and I can't forgive myself for resenting my orphaned nephew, and I can't forgive myself for not being a better sister to Juliet when she needed more of me, not less."

"Which is why you need to forgive yourself. If you can't forgive yourself for being real and human, you'll never be happy."

"I don't deserve to be happy—"

"Of course you do. And I don't know why you feel inadequate, or if you were made to feel inferior as a child, but it's a lie, and a travesty. You are a beautiful, intelligent woman, a passionate loyal woman, and that is rarer and more valuable than the emeralds on your ears."

* * *

The gondola ride was quiet on the return home. Gio said no more than two words during the trip and despite the warmth of her cape, Rachel felt chilled to the core, regretting what she'd told him, wishing she hadn't revealed so much.

Gio took her hand, assisted her from the gondola onto the embankment fronting the palazzo, but didn't let it go, as he walked her inside. As the door shut behind them, he turned her to face him. "Your sister died tragically, and unexpectedly, but you are not to blame for that."

She pushed the hood back on her cape. "She was suffering from postpartum depression—"

"I understand you are grieving for her, but you were not responsible for her—"

"But I *was*—"

"No, and that's the lie. I don't presume to understand all your family dynamics, but you were not put on earth to be your sister's caregiver. You're here to be you, and live your life, and find happiness in your life."

"Maybe. I don't know. But I do know that I can't fail Michael."

For a moment there was just silence, and then Giovanni untied the silk cords on her cape. "You mean, *we*," he corrected. "*We* can't fail him, and *we* have to do better."

He held out his hand to her. "Why don't we go up and check on him together?"

* * *

Reaching the third floor they discovered Michael was asleep in his crib, and Mrs. Fabbro resting in a chair not far away, her hands folded across her middle, her steel-gray head tipped back, eyes closed.

The elderly woman opened her eyes when they approached. Gio spoke quietly to her, and Mrs. Fabbro answered, then with a brief nod and briefer smile in Rachel's direction, she left.

"It was a good night," Gio said to Rachel. "No problems. No fussing. She said he's settling in well here, but thinks we need to think about giving him a proper room."

"I feel badly that we were out so late. Mrs. Fabbro is not a young woman."

"Mrs. Fabbro is delighted to be needed. She would take Michael home and keep him all to herself if she could."

"But I hated seeing her sleeping in a chair."

"If she'd wanted to, she could have slept on the bed. She used to do that with us when we were small and had nightmares."

"Your mother didn't come to you?" she whispered, leaning over the crib to check on Michael.

The baby was fast asleep, his round cheeks rosy. She smiled down at him, thinking he looked like an angel.

Gio reached into the crib and lightly stroked a wisp of Michael's black hair. "If my mother was home, yes. But sometimes she'd travel with my father."

Rachel felt a pang as she saw how gently Giovanni touched their nephew. From the beginning he'd been comfortable holding Michael, and she wondered if he'd had a lot of experience with children, or if he was just a natural. Either way, it was reassuring to see.

Giovanni sighed. "Speaking of Madre, I need to tell you something."

"Is she on her way back home?" she whispered.

"Not exactly." He hesitated. "Come, let's go to my room, and I'll explain all."

It turned out that "Come to my room" didn't mean Gio's office suite, but his bedroom. Rachel felt a flutter of nerves as they entered the high-ceilinged room covered in dark beams with gold stencil, the walls a rustic pumpkin-hued plaster, the bed surprisingly modern and austere with a white linen cover. Two white slipcovered chairs flanked the stone fireplace. Books covered a farmhouse table, with more books stacked on the nightstand next to the low bed.

"Would you like a glass of port?" Gio asked, peeling off his coat.

"I'm good, thank you," she answered, sitting down in one of the chairs by the empty hearth.

"Do you mind if I have one?"

"Of course not."

He went to the long wooden table that nearly

ran the length of the wall and drew the stopper out of the glass decanter and filled a small glass. He turned to face her, his expression shuttered. "Madre doesn't live here anymore. And she's not visiting her sister in Sorrento. She's in a home in Sorrento. I had to make that decision earlier in the year. She has dementia, and it had become too dangerous for her here. I tried my best to keep her here, but there are so many stairs and halls and empty rooms…as well as windows and water." He looked down into his glass. "I did have to fish her out of the lagoon more than once. It was awful. And then she didn't know me."

"I'm sorry."

"She doesn't know about Michael. She doesn't even know that Antonio is gone. She doesn't know any of us anymore—" He broke off, brow furrowing. "I go see her once a month. I know it's not enough, but it is incredibly painful to sit at her side and listen to her ask me over and over who I am." His jaw jutted. "I don't like feeling helpless. And every time I see her, I do."

"I understand," Rachel said softly, and she did.

"I, too, wrestle with guilt. I feel guilty that I am not there with her more, guilty that I wasn't able to keep her here, in her own home. But it hasn't been an easy year. Antonio's death was impossible. It was like a dance step…quick, quick, slow. The diagnosis was quick, and then he was gone to travel and have his last big adventure, and he only returned when he was ready to die, while the actual dying part was brutal and slow." He began unbuttoning his dark shirt. "Once he began dying, it took forever."

"Were you there with him?" Rachel asked, watching his hands work, tackling one button after another.

"Yes. He wanted to die at home—his home, the one in Florence. I was there for the last thirty-five days. I haven't been back in the house since. At some point I need to do something with it, but I have no desire to return anytime soon. Too many memories. Too much suffering."

She felt his pain and it ached within her. "We've both had so much to deal with this year. I feel badly that I judged you—"

"Don't go there. We were both doing the best we could. It wasn't perfect but it was our best. One can't do more than that."

"Yet I always feel as if I *should*."

Shirt unbuttoned, Gio looked at her, his blue gaze intense, the irises bright and hot.

"You set impossible standards for yourself," he said.

"I do," she said softly, thinking she'd never met anyone half so handsome. His cheekbones were high, his eyebrows were straight and black, his jaw was now shadowed, his mouth beautiful.

Her heart thumped as he crossed the room, his shirt open, exposing his broad chest and hard torso, to sit down in the chair opposite her. He was so close now that if she leaned forward she could touch his thigh. Her mouth went dry. She felt positively parched.

"Can I have a sip of your port?" she asked.

He handed her his glass, his fingers brushing hers. She felt a frisson of pleasure all the way through her.

She sipped the warm rich sweet liquor, and then again, welcoming the burst of flavor on her tongue and then the heat that followed, down her throat to seep through her limbs.

She handed the glass back, and then immediately wished she hadn't.

"Come here," he said, gesturing for her. "You're so far away."

"Not that far." Rachel's heart did another painful little beat. "And I think it's safer here."

"There's no canal to fall in. Nothing to hurt you should you lose your balance."

She tried to smile but her throat constricted, her hands balling at her sides, hidden by the gleaming folds of her gorgeous gown. If she let him, he would be her first. And if they married, her first and her last. He would be everything.

"You could hurt me," she said, the words popping out before she could stop them.

He looked relaxed, sitting on the arm of the chair, and yet there was something watchful in his manner. "Why would I do that?"

"We're so different." Her mouth felt dry. "And our dreams are so different."

"I don't know if we are that different. We both value family. We work hard, and try to think of others. We want Michael to be safe, and loved. And we both want to be happy, as well." He smiled a little, but the smile didn't reach his eyes. If anything it emphasized the shadows in the blue depths, the shadows a testament to his grief over losing Antonio.

"Have I missed anything?" he asked quietly.

The fact that he was still grieving for his brother rendered him human, and vulnerable. Yes, he was still impossibly beautiful but he was a man, and he'd hurt, just as she'd hurt. She wanted to comfort him now, but wasn't sure how.

She drew a shallow breath. "Can we both be happy?"

"You mean, together?" he asked.

She nodded.

"If we can move forward together and let the past go."

"It's not easy to let it go, though," she said, nails pressing into her tender palms. "Because you couldn't have saved Antonio, but I could have saved Juliet—" She broke off, chest squeezing, throat tightening, the air trapped in her lungs. She blinked, trying to clear the sting of tears.

"How?" Gio asked, covering her clenched hands with one of his.

"If I'd found all the pills ahead of time. If I'd known she was stockpiling them. If I'd known she was suffering from depression…"

"But you didn't. How could you?"

Rachel's shoulders twisted. "I should have realized she wasn't coping well. In the weeks leading up to her death, she needed more and more help from me, and near the end I had become an almost full-time caregiver." She chewed her lower lip. "I wasn't happy about it. I told her so, too."

"Ah." His hand squeezed hers. "That's why you feel guilty."

"I wish I could go back and do it differently. You have no idea how much I regret those pep talks and lectures. I was trying to help, but I am quite certain they just made her feel worse…they just isolated her further. Rather than giving her tough love, I should have driven her to a doctor."

He tugged her from her chair and pulled her toward him, settling her on his lap. "Hindsight is always clearer," he said gruffly, tilting her chin up to look into her eyes. "But at the time, you didn't know, and you were doing your best."

Rachel bit harder into her lip, fighting to hold back the tears. She hated remembering, and most of all she hated remembering that last night, because every time she thought about that final evening, she thought of everything she should have said or done. "I'm not disappointed in Juliet," she whispered brokenly. "I'm disappointed in *me*."

He kissed her then, his mouth covering hers, his tongue stroking the seam of her lips, until her mouth opened for him. He kissed her with hunger and need and something else she couldn't articulate, and her hands came up to press against his warm, bare chest. He felt good, his skin like satin over dense, hard muscle, and she was torn between pushing him away to preserve her sanity and pulling him closer.

She was sick and tired of fighting herself. Sick and tired of fighting him, and her desire for him. Everything had been so difficult for so long, and she was ready for something else, something new. Could they be happy together? Was it possible that out of all the terrible loss and grief they could create something new?

"I think it's time to take you to bed to stop you from thinking too much," he murmured.

"I am thinking too much," she agreed hoarsely.

"I know the perfect solution for that," he answered, hands sliding into her hair, tilting her head back to give him access to her mouth. He kissed her hard, his tongue first lightly stroking her lips, before finding the roof of her mouth and then the tip of her tongue.

Her pulse jumped and her legs shook as heat flooded her.

The kiss deepened, his tongue taking her mouth, making her melt. Hot sensation rushed through her and her thighs pressed, trying to deny the ache inside her and the way desire coiled within her.

She shuddered as he urged her closer, his strong hand low on her hip, holding her firmly against him, letting her feel his erection. She blushed, and hated herself for blushing. She felt like such a child. It would be a relief to know what to do, to feel confident about herself. Her inexperience had become a problem.

"You're still thinking," he growled in her ear.

"I'm sorry. It's a problem. I'll try to stop—" She broke off as he reached behind her neck and found her zipper.

With practiced ease, he drew the zipper down and slipped the dress off her shoulders. It puddled to her waist.

And then he stood, rising with her in his arms as if she weighed nothing and carried her across the room.

Panic rushed through her, heightening her emotions, making her pulse race even faster. She wanted him and was glad he would be her first, and yet she also worried she'd disappoint him. Should she tell him that she was still a virgin? Did a man want to know something like that? Or would it put too much pressure on him?

He placed her on the bed and her gown slid all the way down, in a pool of shimmering green and gold.

Giovanni's gaze swept over her as she lay before him in her delicate lace bra and matching thong panties. His lashes dropped and his firm lips curved in appreciation. "The things I want to do to you," he said, his voice low.

She exhaled breathlessly, heart pumping so hard she could barely think straight.

Gio joined her on the bed, stretching out over her, his weight braced on his elbows to keep from crushing her. Gazing down into her flushed face, he thought she'd never looked more beautiful. Her dark eyes shone and her soft mouth looked swollen and so incredibly kissable, so kissable that he lowered his head and took her mouth again.

"And Michael? What if he wakes?" Rachel gasped, as he shifted to her neck, kissing down the column to the rise of her collarbone.

He didn't try to answer her immediately, too intent on claiming one lace-covered nipple, his teeth finding the sensitive tip and tugging ever so gently. She gasped again, her body shifting restlessly beneath his.

"Mrs. Fabbro is with him," he answered at length, licking the taut peak, the damp lace imprinting on her tender skin. "She returned to the room after we left, and is sleeping in there with him tonight."

"You didn't say that earlier," she choked, and then arched up as he covered the nipple, sucking again in firm tugs that had her panting, her hands going to his back, her nails pressing against him.

Gio welcomed her sighs of pleasure, just as he welcomed the edge of pleasure and pain as her nails bit into his back. He hadn't wanted to be with anyone this past year. He hadn't wanted intimacy or sex. He hadn't felt desire… He hadn't felt anything, but now he was feeling hunger, desire, need, and he was impatient to have her, impatient to bury himself in Rachel's soft, wet heat.

"Are you on birth control?" he asked, lifting his head.

She shook her head.

"You're not protected?" he repeated, struggling to hold back when all he wanted to do was bury himself inside her.

"No." She drew an unsteady breath. "I've never needed it."

"You leave it to your partner?"

"Yes. No. I mean—" She drew another quick breath, her breasts rising and falling, the dark pink nipples tight buds against the pale creamy skin. "I'm a virgin. I've never needed protection before."

Giovanni stilled, stunned. Was she serious? She was twenty-eight years old, nearly twenty-nine. Were there twenty-nine-year-old virgins out there?

He felt her draw a breath, her rib cage rising and falling. Her voice was tremulous when she spoke. "I realize it's a bit odd, and probably uncomfortable." She inhaled sharply and exhaled, the sound half laugh, half sob. "It's uncomfortable, even for me. I never meant to be this…but here I am. Sexless. Emotionless." Her hand reached out, searching for something to cover herself with.

He rose up, careful not to crush her. "You are not without emotions. You just lack experience. There is a difference."

She said nothing. Her gaze was fixed on a point past his shoulder but he could see the shadows in her eyes, and then came the silent film of tears.

"What happened?" he asked, head dipping to kiss just beneath her jaw, and then another kiss to the tender skin of her throat. "Did someone hurt you? Who broke your heart?"

Her slim shoulder twisted. "No broken heart. I was just holding out for true love. It didn't happen."

"You've never been in love?"

"I think I've come close, but it always ended before I was convinced it was a forever love."

He placed a kiss along her collarbone, and then lower. She shivered and sighed, as he cupped her breast. He eased his hand back and forth over the taut nipple. She inhaled with each stroke, her breathing increasingly shallow.

"And yet you're so sensitive," he murmured, stroking down, his hand caressing the length of her, from her full breast, over her flat stomach to reach the soft mound between her thighs.

"You make me sensitive," she whispered huskily, squirming as he caressed her lightly through the lace panty, light deft touches that made her thighs clench.

"Or maybe you've never given someone the chance to please you." He leaned over and kissed one of her pelvic bones. Her hips rocked against him. He kissed the other and her breath caught in her throat.

"If someone can't please my brain," she choked, "he's not about to get close to my body."

He smiled as his teeth found the edge of elastic bordering her lace thong. "How do you explain us then?"

"You didn't waste time. You went straight for my mind."

He nuzzled her between her thighs, and then traced her with the tip of his tongue. He heard her broken cry as his tongue followed the cleft, the soft shape of her, and then between, where she was so very responsive.

She cried out again when he pushed the scrap of lace aside and touched her with his fingers and tongue, parting her to taste her and tease her. She was tense, nerves wound tight, and trembling as he licked her, slow long flicks of his tongue that had her gasping for air.

Her hips ground up, and he pressed a hand to her tummy, holding her down, holding her still, while he flicked and sucked on her delicate nub, the tender hood hard against his tongue.

"Gio," she choked, her hand reaching for his shoulder, then sliding into his hair.

He could feel her tighten beneath him, feel her

struggling, not wanting to lose control. He eased a finger inside of her, caressing that spot inside her warm slick body and sucked again on her, before gently sliding in another finger, working the inside of her while he matched the pressure on her clit.

She cried out his name as she climaxed, her body tensing, convulsing with pleasure. He held her after, her supple body so warm in his arms.

"That," she whispered, awed, "was amazing."

"Good. But that, *bella*, was just the beginning."

CHAPTER THIRTEEN

RACHEL DIDN'T REMEMBER falling asleep, but when she woke up, she was astonished to discover she was still in Gio's bed, in his room. Morning light streamed through a break in the curtains, streaking the carpeted floor. Memories of last night returned in a rush.

Rachel sat up swiftly, covers clutched to her breasts.

Giovanni reached out and drew her back down. "Where are you going?" he asked, sleepily.

"Michael," she protested, even as Gio pulled her toward him.

"He's with Mrs. Fabbro, remember? I am sure they will be fine for a little bit longer." Gio rolled her onto her back and kissed her, his body hard and warm.

She shivered with pleasure, feeling the thickness of his erection press between her thighs. He'd made her climax twice last night and yet he hadn't taken her virginity. She was ready to lose it. Ready to be his.

"Make love to me," she said, locking her hands around his neck.

"Don't you want to wait for our wedding night?"

"No. It puts too much pressure on the evening. I already feel so much pressure."

"Why?"

She wasn't sure how to explain it to him, but her inexperience was an issue, at least for her. She wanted him, and was glad he would be her first, and yet she was also so very nervous and worried that she'd disappoint him. It was one thing to be a virgin at eighteen, but another at twenty-eight. "What if I'm not any good?" she asked, her voice cracking ever so slightly. "What if you're sorry—"

"You worry far too much about everything. Stop thinking," he said. "Stop analyzing. It's time to live."

"I agree. I want to live. Make love to me. Now. Please."

He rolled her over, so that he was now on the bottom, and she was lying naked on top of him. His hand swept down her bare back, over her hip to tease her bottom. He caressed her like that, once, twice, his touch so light on the curve of her backside, and each brush made more of her nerve endings come to life.

He slid his hands over the curve of her butt again, finding the sensitive crease where her cheeks ended and her leg began. He played with the crease and then the tops of her thighs, stroking out and then in again, melting her from the inside out.

"Please, Gio," she whispered, pressing her pelvis to his, her belly knotting, her womb feeling so empty it made her frantic. She'd waited so long for this, and she was ready. She didn't need more foreplay. She didn't need him to be gentle. She wanted to be taken.

His hand slipped between her thighs, finding her slit. She was hot and wet, and his fingers slipped easily into her, stroking, teasing, before sliding out to spread the moisture over her nub, making her buck.

"Gio," she gritted, arching up as he caressed her again.

He rolled her back over, his knees parting her thighs, holding her open for him. She looked up into his hard, handsome face as she felt the head of his shaft at her entrance. He was smooth and warm and she rubbed herself against him, enjoying the way he felt, and how deliciously sensitive she was with him against her.

He lowered himself to kiss her. "I don't want to hurt you," he said against her mouth.

"It will only hurt the first time, so let's get the first time over."

"My pragmatist," he murmured, smiling. "I appreciate your candor, but it doesn't sound sexy."

"I'm not sexy," she said hoarsely as he shifted,

adjusting himself so that the tip of his shaft was pressing at her entrance.

She exhaled slowly as he pushed in. He was large and she felt tight, but he kept pressing forward, and she drew a deep breath, trying to focus on his warmth and how he felt like satin, but it was snug, as he pushed in, and it began to sting.

Her eyes burned and she blinked, surprised by the pain. She really was too old to be a virgin, she thought blinking back tears.

"I'm hurting you," he said, growing still.

"It's okay," she whispered, her hands sliding around his back, savoring the warmth of his skin and the dense muscle in his back. He did feel good, and she wanted this, and it would only hurt the first time. "Don't stop."

"*Bella*, darling—"

"Please. Don't stop."

He thrust deeply, burying himself in her. Gio kissed her, giving her time to get used to him, and as she responded, kissing him back, he began to move, hips rocking, withdrawing to sink back into her. She felt a sensation that made her sigh, not quite a tickle or tingle, but something almost delicious. He thrust into her again, and she felt the same pleasure. She relaxed, welcoming the press of his body and the way he sank deeply into her. Her pulse quickened as his tempo increased, and she began to breathe more deeply, feeling her body tighten around him. He was driving her toward another orgasm, and she gripped his shoulders, her body lifting to meet his, wanting the pressure and pleasure, wanting him, wanting more of this sensation of them together.

They felt like one. They felt the way she'd thought love would feel. Bright and intense and stunning and so deeply satisfying.

And just like that, she knew two things—she loved him, and she couldn't hold back anymore. She gave in to both then, her heart opening to love him even as her body yielded to the pleasure. She shattered beneath him and kept shattering, and then he, too, must have been climaxing, as he stiffened and his hands buried in her hair, his hard body filling her completely.

For long moments afterward, her heart pumped, and her skin felt hot and flushed. She closed her eyes, savoring the feel of Giovanni and the weight of him on her and in her. It was wonderful. Being with him was wonderful. She knew he didn't love her, and would probably never love her, but in that moment she was happy, genuinely happy, and she laughed out loud, a bright quick gurgle of sound.

Gio lifted his head, looked down at her. "You're laughing?"

"Yes." She smiled up at him, feeling impossibly good, and so very relaxed. "I'm not a virgin anymore, am I?"

"No. Sorry, *bella*, you've been deflowered."

"Thank God! It was about time."

His expression turned wry. "I hope you mean thank God it was with me."

"Well, of course. That, too."

"Hmm."

She snuggled close. "It was amazing, Gio. You were amazing. Thank you."

Later, after their bodies had cooled, Gio kissed her, and then climbed from bed.

"I'll send for coffee," he said.

"Thank you," she said, snuggling down under the covers. "I take it you'll be in your office the rest of the day, doing your usual calls and meetings?"

He paused in the bathroom door, his body beautifully hard and muscular. "In meetings, yes, but these are meetings with you."

"With me?" She propped herself up on one elbow. "Why are we having meetings?"

"I should say appointments. Today is the day we're meeting with the journalist from the big UK magazine, the one that is doing the story on our wedding."

Rachel's smile began to fade. "Gio, not today. Not yet. We haven't even discussed our wedding. We haven't even really planned the engagement party."

"That's just it. I think we should combine them. Why have two events? Why not turn the engagement party into a surprise wedding reception?"

She no longer felt like smiling at all. The big

bubble of happiness inside her had popped, as well. "You're serious, aren't you?"

"There's no reason to drag it out. Let's wed and be done with it—"

"How charming."

"It will be. We can make it fun and today will be fun at any rate. We have a florist coming, and a baker who specializes in wedding cakes."

"I'm surprised you don't have my wedding gown picked out for me."

"I do have a designer coming. She'll have some dresses and sketches."

"Gio, this isn't how a wedding is supposed to work."

"Rachel, we agreed we were going to do what was right for Michael. This is the right thing for him."

She ground her teeth together, holding back tears of frustration.

"*Cara*, darling, we will be happy."

She said nothing, battling the lump filling her throat.

He sighed. "I don't have time to coddle you now. The journalist and her photographer will be here in less than two hours. Do you want me to call in a hair stylist and have someone do your hair for the pictures?"

"I can do it myself."

"Very well. Coffee is on the way. I'm going to shower and shave. Today is about looking happy. Do try to look happy, *bella*, okay?"

Rachel showered and washed her hair, and then while it dried, she spent a half hour with Michael, walking him around the house, showing him all the beautiful things there were to see—chandeliers and Venetian mirrors, gilded frames and oil masterpieces. "This is all your house, too," she told him, struggling to smile, struggling to keep her tone light when her heart felt unbearably heavy because she felt tricked.

Gio had seduced her last night to further his agenda.

It hadn't been a night of mad passion. He hadn't been overcome by emotion. He'd known the reporter was coming today to get their "story" for the magazine, the story being important because it protected Gio's business and all his valuable investors.

She was not important. She was just a means to an end.

Rachel returned Michael to Mrs. Fabbro, and then dressed in her brown lace dress and styled her hair, twisting it up and letting a few tendrils fall free to frame her face.

She could barely stand to look at her reflection. She was too upset, too hurt. Turning from the mirror she headed downstairs, arriving just as the journalist and the photography crew stepped through the front door.

Giovanni made the introductions and ushered everyone into the rose salon with the famous frescoes by Gregorio Lazzarini. The photographer set up his equipment while his assistant arranged the lights and white screen. The English journalist, Heidi Parker, immediately began asking questions, and Gio answered everything she asked with an easy, sexy smile. He looked incredibly comfortable, and when Rachel remained quiet, he slid his arm around her and kissed her on the brow, and then the lips, playing the part of the besotted lover.

"Where will the wedding reception be?" Heidi asked.

"The ballroom," Gio said. "Would you like to see it?"

Heidi nodded and the photographer joined them. Gio opened the doors and stepped back. He didn't need to say or do more. The room spoke for itself, appearing to stretch the length of the house, but that might have been an illusion due to the soaring ceiling with the Baroque frescoes and lavish gold paint.

It wasn't hard to imagine it glittering at nighttime, all five of the lavish chandeliers lit, the crystals gleaming and reflecting light while guests mingled and danced below.

Rachel's heart ached as Gio shared some of the wedding details. It would be without a doubt the most beautiful and fashionable event of the year. The reception would be extravagant, and Giovanni would serve the Marcello wine from his vineyard.

But it wasn't the kind of wedding she wanted. She didn't want a show. She didn't want fuss and extravagance. She wanted something intimate and warm and full of love.

They left the ballroom and headed for the dining room, which had been turned into a floristry. Flowers were everywhere, in buckets and vases, in hand-tied bouquets and elegant boutonnieres. The bouquets were lush and wildly romantic and Rachel found herself lifting one and smelling it, and then froze when she realized the photographer was clicking away, capturing her with the pink roses and peonies and lilies.

"Beautiful," the photographer said, giving her a smile.

It was all she could do not to cry when Gio pulled her into his arms and kissed her, giving the photographer another "candid" shot, and then Gio was sharing more details about their guest list and who had been invited. They were all society people, and Heidi scribbled away, murmuring about what a spectacular event it would be, such an A-list party.

The very description sent a chill through Rachel. She was not an A-lister herself. She was not even close to a B-or C-list.

Gio was right. She was firmly middle class. A woman from Burien, Washington who had to struggle for everything in life.

"How does it feel knowing that you will have

the wedding of the year?" Heidi asked Rachel. "Is it at all intimidating?"

"Very much so," Rachel answered, voice wobbling. "Giovanni's friends are powerful and influential…aristocrats, millionaires and billionaires, race car drivers, fashion designers, models, actors and socialites…" Her voice faded, the stream of words ending. "Not my sort of people at all," she concluded unsteadily, aware that Heidi and the photographer had just exchanged curious glances.

Giovanni didn't seem disturbed. He kissed the top of her head. "My sweet bride."

Heidi scribbled something. "And the baby?" she asked. "Will we meet him? Do say yes. We are so hoping for a picture of the three of you."

"No. We're determined to protect his privacy," Gio answered firmly. "It was the one condition we had about the interview. The focus would be Rachel and me. It's not fair to Michael to put him in the limelight."

Heidi nodded. "Of course. And I did know. But what kind of journalist would I be if I didn't try?"

Gio gestured toward the door. "I believe our chef is here. Shall we go discuss our wedding cake?"

While Heidi stayed back with the photographer, helping hold one temperamental light, Rachel moved close to Gio, whispering to him as they exited the dining room. "You seem to be quite enjoying the fuss."

"It's for the cameras."

She shot him a dubious glance. "I don't believe you."

He glanced back at Heidi, who was now bustling toward them. His broad shoulders shifted. "I want a wedding to remember."

"Funny, but I want a wedding I can forget."

"You've lost your sense of humor, Rachel. Why can't you have fun with this? Why not enjoy planning the wedding?"

"Because it seems like a terrible extravagance!"

"Maybe I see this as the right opportunity to return to society."

"The right opportunity being before the stock offerings," she said under her breath.

But he heard her. He lifted a brow. "My goal is to protect all. The company. The employees. The family. Michael." He reached out and tipped her chin up, his gaze locking with hers. "You."

"I'm not a Marcello."

"Not yet in name, but in body, I've already claimed you."

Her heart hurt and heat washed through her. "You have no idea how much I regret that, too."

He gave her a look. "I don't believe that, and neither do you."

With that, he headed into the palazzo's vast kitchen, a room that might have been medieval at one point, but was a stunning space of light and gleaming white marble.

Like the dining room that had been filled with flowers, the long white marble counters were filled with cakes. Tall, white, layered cakes and large square cakes covered in sugared fruit. There was a cone cake with caramel-covered pastries and puffs of whipped cream and a chocolate something with more whipped cream.

The photographer immediately wanted photos, and Heidi went over to introduce herself to the chef.

Giovanni leaned against a white counter, arms folded across his chest. "You must admit this is an easy way to do an interview," he said as Rachel reluctantly came to stand at his side. "We're giving them a show, but we're not having to tell them very much about us."

"I'd like to give them a show, but it would involve smashing cake in your face."

He laughed softly. "You are determined to be angry."

"You should have told me last night that the reporter was coming this morning. It would have changed things."

"How so?"

I wouldn't have given you my heart, she thought, looking away, jaw grinding to hold back the emotion, *I would have just given you my body.* But Rachel wasn't sure that was true. She didn't think she could have helped falling for him. And maybe that was why she was angry. She'd wanted to hold out for true love. Instead she'd fallen for Gio.

He tipped her chin up. "It wouldn't have changed anything, *cara*. You willingly, happily went to bed with me last night. I kissed every inch of your lovely body, and then this morning, after a good sleep, when you couldn't blame the wine for clouding your judgment, I took your virginity. There was no coercion involved."

"Can you not say *virginity* so loud?" she gritted, face on fire.

"Is that why you're so sensitive this morning? Did you want to lounge around this morning—"

"No."

"Savoring your first time?"

She dug her nails into her palms. "I will slap you if you continue mocking me."

"I am not mocking you."

"Then what are you doing?"

"Teasing you." He leaned forward and kissed her brow. "As new lovers do," he added with another kiss. Gio drew back and smiled into her eyes. "Shall we go select our wedding cake?"

The chef had a speech prepared, and in the palazzo's cavernous kitchen, he shared how cake wasn't just something sweet with which to finish the meal, but the breaking of bread over the bride's head dated to the ancient Romans. The groom would smash the cake—sometimes even throw it at her—as a fertility ritual.

Rachel's lips compressed. "What a lovely thing

for a man to do to his bride," she said under her breath. "I'm sure she enjoyed it immensely."

Gio grinned lazily at her. "Is that your sense of humor returning?"

"Oh no. It's gone. I don't think it'll ever be back, either."

He just laughed, and the photographer snapped away, and the chef kept talking as he showed them each of the different types of cake they could choose for their wedding.

"This is the classic Italian white cake," he said, gesturing to a four-tier cake. "It is the one most similar to your American wedding cake style. In Italy, the beautiful white icing represents purity and fidelity, and the bride's faithful devotion to her new husband."

"That sounds like our perfect cake," Gio said.

Rachel shot him a dark glance. "What other choices do we have?"

The chef went on to the next cake. "Many couples choose *millefoglie*, a very traditional cake comprised of very thin, delicate layers of pastry with a light cream mascarpone filling. *Millefoglie* translates to 'a thousand layers' and is finished with powdered sugar and fresh berries. You can also choose a chocolate cream filling instead of mascarpone if you are a chocolate fan." The chef smiled. "The only drawback to such a cake is that it cannot be stacked, so it does not create quite the same centerpiece effect."

"Since my bride is American, I think we should give her a tall cake," Gio said.

The chef moved to the third cake. "There is also the profiterole cake. It is a tower cake, but instead of layers of cake that have been iced and stacked, it is a cone covered in cream-filled pastries. It is a very European cake, popular in France, too, although there it is called *croquem-bouche*."

The room was silent as everyone looked at her, as if eager for her pronouncement. "I don't care," Rachel whispered, overwhelmed. "Whatever Giovanni wants. This is his big day, too."

Gio's gaze met hers and held. "I think we should go with the traditional layered cake," he said after a moment. "A white layered cake with all white frosting to symbolize my beautiful bride's purity and devotion."

And then it was all over. The photographer and journalist left, and the chef packed up his cakes, and it was just Rachel and Gio with a stack of sketches—the wedding dresses.

Rachel numbly leafed through the illustrations of gorgeous white dresses but they were all just that—formal white gowns that meant nothing to her. She was finding it impossible to wrap her head around the marriage and the wedding and everything else. Finally, she just pushed the sketches across the table to Gio. "You decide," she said. "I don't care. I really don't."

* * *

It wasn't the answer Gio wanted, but he smiled lazily, hiding his frustration. But later, when he was in his office, he found himself pausing between conference calls to wonder why he wanted her to care. He wanted her to be enthusiastic; he wanted the wedding ceremony and reception to be something they'd both enjoy, and he wasn't sure why.

They weren't marrying out of love. This was a practical marriage at best. So why should it matter if she was or wasn't excited about the ceremony? Why should he want her to treat this as if it was her dream wedding?

Why did he want her to be happy about marrying him?

Maybe it was because he was actually quite happy with her. He liked her, a great deal as a matter of fact.

He liked looking at her and he thoroughly enjoyed touching her and tasting her and giving her pleasure. He even found himself wanting to hold her, and since Adelisa, he hadn't wanted to hold any woman, not after sex. Usually after his orgasm, he was done. Physically satisfied and ready to move on to the next thing. But with Rachel in his bed, the orgasm was just the beginning. The orgasm was almost incidental. There was something about her warmth and softness that made him want to stay with her, keeping her close, kissing her and exploring her sweet curves, and then making love all over again.

With her in his bed, he felt relaxed and settled. Calm. Peaceful. Yes, that was it. Peaceful. She fit in his life. She fit in his arms and, indeed, in his heart.

He wasn't one to use flowery phrases and spout poetry, and he didn't glorify romantic love, but some part of him believed that marrying might just possibly be the smartest thing he'd ever do, and not simply because it'd keep her and Michael in Venice, but because it'd give him a strong, independent and self-sufficient partner. A partner he could trust.

But she needed to trust him. And be happy with him.

Rachel entered the smaller salon, which had been turned into a dining room for them that evening. In front of the marble hearth, a table had been set for two, with a high chair placed between the two dining chairs.

Seeing the antique wooden high chair at the table put a lump in Rachel's throat. The chair was so ornate, probably a family heirloom, and it made the dining table look cozy and domestic.

Moments later Gio entered the room with Michael in his arms and she had to blink back tears.

"I thought it was time we had a family dinner," Gio said, giving her a smile that made her heart turn over. Michael babbled something and took his fist from his mouth and bounced it on Gio's freshly shaven cheek. Gio grinned and his quick flash of white teeth made everything inside her chest tighten and ache.

Gio looked beyond gorgeous tonight, and his ease with Michael made her want to weep. How was she going to resist a man who loved children?

"You don't mind that I wanted him to join us, do you?" Gio asked, looking from Michael to her.

"No, of course not," she answered quickly, breathlessly. "In Seattle, he's my dinner date every night." She couldn't quite get over Gio's ease with Michael, though. He looked incredibly comfortable and it didn't make sense. He was supposed to be this cold, unfeeling man, and yet he was carting around the six-month-old as if they were lifelong friends. "Have you had a lot of experience with babies and children?"

"None. Does it show?"

"No. You're a natural."

"I think it helps that I like him," he answered, glancing down at the baby, but she heard the way his voice deepened. She heard the rasp of emotion. Gio loved Michael.

"He reminds you of your brother, doesn't he?" she said.

"Yes. It's bittersweet, but definitely more sweet

than bitter." He hesitated. "Do you see your sister in him?"

"No. Not at all. He is very much a Marcello."

"So you don't hate all Marcellos."

She felt another pang. "I don't hate you, Gio," she whispered, because she didn't. She couldn't. Not when she'd begun to care so very much. Somehow in the past four days he'd become not just familiar, but *hers*. Her Giovanni Marcello, her impossible Venetian.

Or maybe she felt like his. He was making her his, and she was finding it hard, if not impossible, to resist.

"Good, because Michael and I have a question for you." Shifting the baby, Gio reached into his coat and withdrew a small black ring box.

Her heart did another funny dip. She knew what this was.

He could see that she knew, too, and his lips curved ever so faintly. Gio walked toward her and Michael batted the velvet box. Rachel couldn't move, rooted to the spot.

Reaching her side, he opened the top revealing an enormous, intense yellow, square-cut diamond ring surrounded by smaller white diamonds, but he wasn't looking at the ring. He was looking into her face, his gaze holding hers. "*Bella* Rachel, marry me."

He'd been calling her *bella* for the past few days, and she'd thought she knew what it meant—

beautiful—but she wasn't beautiful. Juliet was beautiful. Rachel knew she bordered on plain. "Please don't mock me," she whispered.

"Why can't you be beautiful?" he asked. "Why must you assume I'd want someone like your sister? Yes, she caught Antonio's eye, but she's not the kind of woman I'm drawn to. You are. You are my idea of beautiful."

"You say that because you never met her."

"You don't think I've had my pick of beautiful women? I'm thirty-eight. I'm wealthy. I can support any woman in any lifestyle she wants. Trust me, women are drawn to me, but I want you, *bella*. I'm drawn to *you*."

She swallowed hard. "Do you mind terribly that I'm not interested in your money? And that I am not very interested in having a lifestyle? I just want to be a good mother to Michael, and hopefully, a good wife to you."

"Does that mean you'll accept Michael's and my proposal?"

He hadn't mentioned love, but then, she didn't expect him to. Right now she didn't need the word when she felt his strength and passion and commitment. She believed he would be a good husband. A kind husband. And an honest one, too.

"Yes." She smiled shyly. "Can I put on the ring?"

"If you don't mind that Michael's begun to drool all over it."

"That's his seal of approval, you know," she

answered, holding her hand out so that Gio could slide the stunning yellow diamond onto her finger.

"My beautiful funny Rachel," Gio said, putting the ring on her finger, where it glinted with fire and light. He shifted Michael and kissed her, and then again. "I am so glad your sense of humor is back. You make me smile and laugh. It has been such a long time since I did either."

She reached up and touched his jaw, her fingernails lightly raking his jaw. "So you appreciate my brains and beauty."

"All of it. And all of you. I love your eyes and how they show everything you're thinking and feeling. I love your mouth—you have perfect lips—and I love that when I kiss you, you make this little whimper. I find that incredibly sexy."

And then he kissed her and his kiss lit her up like a Christmas tree. "I can't wait until bedtime," she whispered.

"I can't, either, as I intend to show you something new tonight, something guaranteed to give you intense pleasure."

"Don't tease."

"I'm not. It's a promise."

CHAPTER FOURTEEN

RACHEL LOOKED AT herself in the floor-length mirror. Her figure-hugging wedding gown was made of white lace, and the lace hugged her curves before billowing out just above the knees. The lace sleeves were long, reaching the back of her hand, and the fitted lace collar high. Her veil, made of the same lace, covered her from head to toe.

She'd been dressed as if she was still the virgin bride, although she was far from virginal now.

As she put on one of the diamond earrings Gio had given her for an early wedding gift, she told herself she was happy. She was marrying someone whom she was compatible with. Indeed, with him she experienced incredible pleasure. She hadn't even imagined that she could feel so much, never mind the sizzling, dazzling heat that burned in her veins and hummed in her body making her reckless with need.

Of course she wished Gio loved her. She wished he felt for her even half of what she felt for him.

Maybe that's why the sex was so good. It wasn't just sex for her. It was love. When she gave herself to him each night—and morning—she gave herself completely, not just her body, but her soul and heart.

She was lucky to have a good partner, someone to help her raise Michael, someone who would treat Michael as his own son, but still—*still*—it would have been even better, it would have been perfect, if that someone loved *her*.

Earrings in place, she turned away from the mirror and was preparing to leave when a knock sounded at the door, and then her bedroom door opened, and it was Gio.

"What are you doing here?" she said, unable to hide herself. "It's bad luck for a groom to see the bride on the wedding day."

"I have something for you," he said, entering her room with a large leather box.

"You've already given me these gorgeous earrings."

"This is different."

That's when she saw his expression. Something was wrong. Gio wasn't smiling. He looked somber and hard and impossibly remote. Her heart did a painful little beat.

"What is that box?" she asked. The dark box was the size of a loaf of bread, and the polished surface gleamed, the exterior made of inlaid wood, the wood carved into an intricate design of flowers and fruits and musical instruments. It looked old, hundreds of years old, and valuable.

Rachel suspected it'd been designed to hold jewelry or a dagger or something else of value.

"You need to have a look at what's inside."

"Now?"

"Yes."

"Will it take long? We're supposed to be getting married soon."

He carried the box to her bed and placed it on the white coverlet. "I want you to see this before we do. I think it's important…for you. For us."

It was in that moment, when he sounded so distant and grave, that she realized how much she loved him, and how much she wanted to be his wife, and how very much she wanted a happy future with him.

She realized in that moment that she could lose everything, and didn't want to lose everything. Gio didn't love her, but he was good to her, and kind. Fearless and strong.

Deep down she hoped—believed—she could get him to love her one day. That one day they would both be happy, together.

"Why do this now?" she whispered. "You must have a reason."

"I do."

"It can't be good. From your expression, it's not good."

"I just need you to know what I know. And then we will marry, and we will raise Michael together, and all will be well."

But he didn't believe it, she thought. And that was what terrified her.

"Please," Gio said, tapping the box.

Rachel crossed the room and sat down on the bed. As she lifted the box, Gio moved away, going to stand at the windows. She glanced at his rigid back, and then opened the box. The lid was hinged and when lifted, she saw the interior was filled with envelopes and papers.

Rachel carefully lifted the paperwork out and scanned the envelopes and printed emails, shivering as she recognized her sister Juliet's handwriting. The letters and cards and emails were all from Juliet to Antonio.

She took the top envelope. The date on the postmark was December 31. She looked behind that one. The postmark was December 25. The envelope behind that one was postmarked December 18.

The letters went all the way back to May 19, the day Antonio died.

Pulse racing, insides churning, Rachel reached for the letter at the very bottom, the one postmarked May 19, and opened the letter and began to read.

My dearest Antonio,
How dare you leave me? How dare you go? I need you so much. I don't know how to do this without you. I love you too much. I have always loved you too much. We both know it.

It frightens me that I love you more than life itself. And now you're gone without even a last goodbye and it's not fair. You've never been fair. You swept me off my feet and made me believe in love and miracles. You seemed like a miracle.

You allowed me to dream and hope and believe, and now you tell me that you're sick, and dying, and you should have told me first. You should have told me before I gave you my heart and soul.

Rachel's hands were shaking so hard she couldn't see the next line and she paused, glancing blindly up. "I don't understand," she whispered.

"You will," Gio said.

Gulping a breath, Rachel returned to the letter.

I don't know how to raise this baby without you. I didn't want to be a mother. I wanted to be your wife, your woman, your lover. And now I've a child but not you.

You have broken my heart.

You have broken me.

Yours forever and ever,

Juliet

Rachel's hands shook as she folded the letter back up and slid it into the envelope. A tear fell and she knocked it away as she returned the envelope to the bottom of the pile. She couldn't bring herself to read more.

"Why did you bring these to me?" she choked.

"They are all like that." Giovanni spoke from across the room.

Rachel drew a deep raw breath and then another. "You've read them all?"

"Not all. Maybe a quarter, if that. It didn't feel right to continue reading when they were not meant for me."

"When did you read these? Have you had these all this time?" Rachel struggled to stop the tears but they kept falling.

"Mrs. Fabbro brought the box with her when his Florence home was closed. She used to work for him in Florence, and when the letters arrived from Juliet, she'd put them in this box. She gave me the box several days ago, and I finally had a chance to go through the letters last night." He hesitated. "I couldn't sleep afterward."

"You should have woken me."

"But then you wouldn't be able to sleep, either."

Her eyes continued to burn. She blinked. "She really loved him."

"Yes. I didn't believe her, but I do now."

"She wasn't as shallow as you thought."

Gio was silent. "There is something I haven't told you. I need to tell you." He glanced at her over his shoulder, expression grim. "Antonio loved your sister, too. He didn't leave her because he didn't care. He left her because he didn't want her to see him die. He left her to protect her from the ugliness of his death."

"How do you know?"

"He left her his entire estate. His homes, his assets, his stock in Marcello SpA. All of it."

"What?"

"He didn't leave her penniless. He left her a very wealthy woman, setting her up so that she could raise his son properly, wanting his woman and his child provided for."

Rachel wanted to move but her legs wouldn't stand. She sat, hands clasping the box, heart on fire. "I don't understand. But she received nothing. She didn't know—"

"She was never told."

"How? Why not?"

"I took legal action when his will was revealed, petitioning our courts to investigate the legality of the document." Gio stood before her, handsome in his tuxedo, but utterly unrepentant. "He had an inoperable tumor in his brain. He was dying. His behavior had become increasingly erratic. I was concerned he was being played, or coerced, and so I asked the courts to intervene—"

"Causing my sister's death," she interrupted hoarsely.

"Your sister didn't want his money, she wanted him."

"How do you know?"

"She refused it. She rejected every bank wire he sent her. Finally, near the end of his life, he simply changed his will."

"And you knew all of this, the entire time?"

"I've learned bits and pieces over time, but yes, I've known since his will was read last June that he left her virtually his entire estate."

Rachel rose, legs and body trembling. She was shaking from her head to the tips of her white silk high-heeled shoes. "You've known since Michael's birth that Antonio wanted to provide for his child, and indeed, tried to provide but you interfered. You withheld support, and not just support, but *love.*"

"I did what I thought was right," he answered tersely.

"But it wasn't right, and you…you don't know the first thing about love. You have no idea what love means, or you wouldn't have worried more about your Marcello stock and investments than your late brother's child!"

"I was wrong, Rachel."

"You….you…" She shook her head, eyes burning, chest so tight she couldn't breathe. "You're not just wrong. You're not even the man I thought you were, Giovanni. You're not at all the man—" She turned away to cover her face with her hands. She pressed her fists against her eyes, holding back the scalding tears, and the grief, and the pain.

Gio had lied to her. *Lied.* Nothing about their

relationship was true. He was false, and selfish, and incapable of caring for anyone but himself. Incapable of loving.

"Thank God you told me now," she said, choking on a muffled sob. "Thank God I found out before it was too late."

"We're still going to marry, Rachel. We still need to protect Michael."

She nearly lost it then. "You're the last one I'd trust to protect Michael! You've done everything in your power to punish him—"

"I had to be cautious."

"Of course you'd see it that way. I don't. But what I do see is the light, and the truth, and the exit, because I want out. I'm not going to do this. I don't have to do this with you, not anymore. You see, Gio, I don't benefit from marrying you. I don't win anything. I just lose. I lose out on the opportunity to be cherished and loved. And it's not worth it—"

"What about Michael?"

"I love Michael, and will always love him, but we don't need you. We don't need your help. I don't want anything to do with you. Keep your precious Marcello stock. Keep your Marcello name." She glanced down at the huge yellow diamond weighting her hand. She'd thought it absolutely beautiful when he'd put it on her finger but now it symbolized all that she hated. Rachel tugged the ring off and dropped it on the bed,

next to the antique wood box. "And your Marcello jewels."

"You don't mean that, *cara*."

"Oh, but I do." Hands shaking, Rachel took off
one earring and then the next and tossed them
onto the bed, too. "I'll take Michael back to Seattle with me, and I shall raise Michael myself,
and he'll be a Bern, and he'll be loved and we
might struggle, but at least we'll struggle with
love, away from your contempt, and condemna-
tion, and judgment."

Gio crossed the room and caught her by the
arm, pulling her toward him. "I understand why
you're upset. I was upset last night, too—"

"For different reasons, I imagine."

"No, for the same reasons. My brother loved
your sister, and they had a tragic love story, and
a tragic ending, but we are not going to continue
the tragedy. It ends here. It ends now. Michael was
a true love child, and he shall be brought up with
love, not fear or shame."

She yanked away and, taking several steps
back, began unpinning the veil, not caring that
it was tearing at her elegant chignon. "I would
never shame him! You're the one that withheld
support because you doubted the legitimacy of
your brother's love."

"My brother was not himself at the end. The
tumor was impacting critical thinking, and he
made a number of rash decisions. After his death

I was inundated with crises, all requiring my attention as well as that of Marcello's legal team. I wasn't even aware of Michael's existence until my private investigators informed me just before Christmas that your sister had given birth in September and had put my brother's name on the birth certificate."

"So why didn't you reach out to my sister then?" she demanded fiercely.

Gio didn't answer and she swallowed around the lump filling her throat. Her voice was hoarse when she added, "Because you thought she was a gold digger and you were not going to reward her."

"You admit your sister's history was problematic, and I wanted to have a DNA test done to see if the baby was truly my brother's—"

"That was December," she said, balling the long lavish lace veil and throwing it at him. It fell short, though, fluttering to the ground. "This is March. DNA tests do not take three months. And the drag…the excessive amount of time wasn't due to the investigation, it's due to your own blindness because you were duped by a gold digger, and so you assume every woman is a gold digger. This isn't even about Juliet and Antonio… it's about you!"

"Not true."

"Oh, it is true, absolutely."

"Rachel, your sister was not the only one to

claim to have borne my brother a child. Your sister was one of dozens."

"I don't believe you."

"Over the years many women have claimed to be pregnant, demanding financial support, or worse, a wedding ring. All were eventually proven false. Until Juliet." He drew a breath, features taut. "Money makes people do stupid things."

"Yes, it does," she shot back, growing angrier, not calmer. "And it's made you selfish and cynical and hard. You think the worst of people, not the best. But once you knew the truth about Juliet, you owed it to her to reach out and do what was right. You *owed* it to her and Antonio to make amends."

"I would have eventually," he answered quietly.

"Eventually," she repeated, voice strangled. *"Eventually* killed her, Gio."

"Money wouldn't have changed her mental state, Rachel. Clearly, she wasn't well if you— who were *there*—couldn't help her. How could I?"

"You accept no blame, do you?"

"My job was to protect my family, including the business, a business that employs thousands of people. To give a quarter of a billion-dollar company to a young woman halfway across the world without doing due diligence, could have meant the end of Marcello Enterprises—"

"It's always about the business, isn't it?"

"I was raised from birth to put the family business first."

"I think you mean from birth you were raised to put the business first. Family appears to be a very distant second."

"I won't apologize for being skeptical. I thought your sister took advantage of a dying man, and I wasn't about to see his estate go to someone who hadn't loved him, but rather saw an opportunity to grow rich at someone else's expense. I will apologize for the lengthiness of the investigation. I insisted it be thorough, but I realize now that my legal team was perhaps too meticulous—"

"You can't even apologize without adding in disqualifiers."

"I'm sorry your sister is dead, but my brother is gone, too." His voice was deep and granite hard, and yet his accent softened the words, taking the truth and pain in them and searing them into her heart. "They're both gone," he added, "but they're not lost to us. They've left us their love child."

"Stop. You don't love, and you don't believe in love."

"That's not true. I love you—"

"*Now* you say it? Now, when it's all over? When it's too late? My goodness, you're desperate—"

He moved while she was speaking, reaching for her, bringing her hard against him. He cupped her face and kissed her, a kiss that was unlike any of the kisses before. This one wasn't hard and fierce, nor was it scalding, blistering with bone-melting desire. This kiss was dark and in-

tense, layered with emotion and raw, undeniable
need. He didn't just want her lips and touch. She
felt as if he wanted to reach into her and steal her
very heart.

"You can't have me," she whispered against his
mouth, as tears stung her eyes and filled the back
of her throat. "You Marcellos have taken enough."
She wrenched away and nearly tripped over her
full lace skirt in her need for distance. "It's over,
Gio. We're through—"

"Not by half," he ground out. "We have a family."

"You're not part of it anymore."

"It doesn't work that way. You can't cut me out.
Your sister didn't leave a will. She didn't indicate
that she wanted you to be Michael's guardian. You
have no more legal right to him than I do."

"But I want him more."

"That's not true. I want him very much. He's all
I have left of my brother, which makes him infi-
nitely dear. Unlike you and Juliet, I didn't have a
complicated relationship with Antonio. There was
no guilt or anger, no envy or resentment. From
the time he was born, he was my brother and best
friend. I sat with him as he died, and it killed me
watching him suffer and fade. His death wasn't
quick, either. It took him weeks to go, and even
as great as his suffering was, I grieved terribly
when he was gone. I still miss him profoundly."

His words came at her, one after the other, and

it was overwhelming his passion and love—love he'd never shown her. She shouldn't be jealous, but she was. Rachel had wanted Gio to love her that much, but he never did.

"No, I didn't rush to Seattle with open arms when I learned of Michael," Gio added. "But I had to be cautious about this claim that he had a son there. A dozen different women claimed they'd had his son or daughter. A dozen different claims to process. A dozen different women who wanted a piece of Antonio's wealth. It was bad enough to lose my brother, but then to deal with all of this desperation and greed?"

Rachel flinched, aware of how desperate she'd been when she'd arrived in Venice on Gio's doorstep. "Desperation doesn't make a person bad!"

"No, but it does make one suspect."

"You should have told me this right away. You should have sat me down on that first day in your mother's favorite salon and laid out the facts—"

"*Buon Dio*, Rachel! You had called the paparazzi. You invited the media to my doorstep. How was I to trust you?"

She shook her head, thoughts muddled, hating that he could tangle her up, make her question everything all over again.

Gio closed the distance, hands settling on her shoulder, his skin so warm through the thin lace of her gown. "We have both made our share of mistakes, but we won't make another one today.

We will marry, and we will be a family for Michael. You may feel hurt, and you might be angry with me, but you can't allow your anger to hurt Michael. *Our* baby."

Our baby. The words rippled through her, and she exhaled at the truth in the words. Gio somehow always cut straight to the heart. Maybe it was his engineering mind, or maybe it was his way of problem solving, but it felt as if he'd taken a lance to her, cutting away the garbage and nonsense and revealing what was essential and true.

Michael was theirs. He wasn't Juliet's any longer, nor was he Antonio's.

They were both gone. They would never return.

"We will love him and protect him," Gio said, one hand slipping up over her neck, his fingers spreading across her jawbone, cradling her face as if a jewel or flower. Every place he touched tingled, her skin flushed and sensitive. "We will not be destructive or selfish. We will put aside our differences and do right by our son."

She stared up into Gio's brilliant blue eyes, seeing him, all of him, not just his dark good looks, but his heart. His fierce, hard heart. He was brutal and relentless and he'd smashed her hopes and dreams. "I loved you," she said numbly. "And I gave you my heart, but I've taken it back. It's not yours. It will never be yours again."

His thumb stroked her cheek as it met the edge

of her mouth. "We can work through this. And we will, after the wedding."

Her lips quivered at the caress. He stroked down again, lingering at the curve of her mouth. She didn't know where to look. She certainly couldn't look into his eyes, not anymore, and so she stared at his mouth and chin, her chest filled with rage and pain. Why had she ever come to Italy? Why had she thought that Giovanni would be the help she needed? She closed her eyes to keep tears from forming. "I won't forgive you."

"It's not as bad as that, *il mio amore*."

"It is as bad as that," she corrected, trying to pull away.

He didn't let her. He held her, and then he pressed a kiss to her forehead, the kiss careful, gentle, far too kind. "Our guests are waiting. I will help you put your veil back on, and then let's go finish what we have begun."

CHAPTER FIFTEEN

SHE FELT WOODEN during the twenty-minute ceremony, and then dead during the reception.

It was all a blur. The meal. The toasts. The music. The cake.

She didn't even remember stepping on to the ballroom floor for their dance. She couldn't feel her legs. Couldn't feel anything but Gio's hand on her side, his hand on her back, his hand on her arm as he steered her here and there, from one place to another, keeping her moving, keeping up appearances, keeping it together.

And then finally, finally it was over and she was in her room, but it wasn't her room anymore. During the reception someone had emptied the wardrobe in the blue guest room and taken everything out, taking all of her things out, putting them elsewhere.

Rachel sank onto her bed, the bed that was no longer her bed, her white full skirts pillowing up, and then fluttering down.

She didn't have anything anymore. She wasn't even herself anymore.

The door opened and closed. She knew without looking that it was Gio. She could feel his energy and intensity from across the room.

"This isn't your room anymore," he said quietly.

Hot tears filled her eyes. "You've taken everything from me."

"But I've also given everything to you. My home, my name, my heart—"

"You don't have a heart."

He didn't answer, not right away. He walked around the perimeter of the room, studying the blue silk wall covering and the enormous gold framed mirror and then the blue painted dresser with the pair of blue vases.

"If that was true, then I wouldn't feel anything right now," he said, lifting one of the blue vases and turning it in his hands. "I wouldn't care so very much that I've hurt you. And I wouldn't mind that you're in here, alone, feeling betrayed and deceived." He set the vase back down and faced her. "But I do mind very much. It wounds me that I've hurt you and ruined your wedding day—"

"Please stop. You're just making it worse. I don't want to talk to you. I don't want to see you. I just want to go home, to Seattle."

"But this is your home now."

"No."

"Yes. And we are a family now."

"Never!"

"And my wife, whom I love."

She covered her ears and squeezed her eyes shut, refusing to listen, unable to endure any more. He'd won. Couldn't he see that he'd won? Did he have to break her completely? "Then prove it," she cried, jumping up. "Prove you love me. Do what's best for me. Let me go."

He stood before her, expression shuttered. "Giving up on you, giving up on us, doesn't prove love. It shows defeat."

"I'm not a challenge. I'm not a business deal."

"I know. You're my wife."

"But I don't want to be your wife, not like this, and for me, this…" She gestured to the room, the house, the city beyond the windows, "This will never be okay."

She had to go. She had to get out of here. She'd leave everything behind. She didn't need her clothes, or her suitcase. She just needed her passport. "I'm leaving," she said hoarsely. "Tonight. I don't want anything from you. I don't want money. I just want my passport so I can go."

"What about Michael's?"

"I'm not taking him with me. He will stay here with you for now, but I'm hiring an attorney. I'm going to sue for custody—"

"It could take years, and I'm not sure you'd win."

"What else am I to do? Stay here and pretend that you didn't lie to me and manipulate me?"

"I'm asking you to forgive me. I'm asking you to understand that I was in a difficult position, too."

"I was not a gold digger!" She threw the words at him, eyes brilliant with unshed tears. "I never wanted your money. I wanted *you*."

"Good. Because I want you. Not just want you. I need you." He hesitated. "I need you with me."

"You don't mean it. You can't even say the words without flinching."

"It's true. I don't speak of love easily, and until tonight, I have never told any woman I loved her. Just as you refused to make love until you had found the right one, I have held out, too. There are only a few people in my life that I can say I truly love. My mother. My brother. Michael. And you." He approached her. "Yes, *you*. I love you, Rachel."

"You're only saying that because you're desperate."

"You're absolutely right. I am desperate. I'm desperate for you to stay. I'm desperate to salvage what's left of our wedding day. Today was horrendous, but we still have the night—"

"No."

"Yes. We have the night, and we have every night from now on. I'm not going to let you go. This is your home now. You belong here, with me." He moved toward her, a slow walk to match his measured words. "Rachel, I didn't have to marry."

"But you did. The media...the company going public...you couldn't have the scandal."

"Money is money. I have plenty of it, but money doesn't buy happiness and I would never, ever marry just to protect my financial interests or investments."

"But you said—"

"It was a tactic." He shrugged, unrepentant. "I wanted you here. I wanted you with me. And yes, I want Michael, but I want you every bit as much. From the moment you appeared on my doorstep, you've been mine. I waited thirty-eight years to find someone like you. You can't think I'm just going to give you up?"

Her head spun. He was saying the right words, all the things she'd wanted him to say, but why did he wait so long? Why hadn't he shared all of this before? "You just don't want me to go."

"You're right. I didn't marry you in an extravagant, romantic wedding to lose my bride before the honeymoon."

She drew a quick, sharp breath. "There will be no honeymoon."

"Of course there will, but there won't be if you leave."

He was trying a new tactic, she thought, and she didn't want to be intrigued but she couldn't help showing a little interest. "Why haven't you mentioned it before?" she asked suspiciously.

"Because it was supposed to be a surprise."

She wished she wasn't curious. She wished she didn't care. But she did care, not about the trip, but about what he might have planned for her. For them. "Where were we going to go?"

"Ravello, on the Amalfi Coast."

Rachel drew a quick, shallow breath, feeling far too many emotions, not the least being regret. "Were we going to take Michael?"

"No. Not on our honeymoon. I wanted time alone with you, my bride, my wife, my heart." He reached for her and drew her toward him, little by little, step by step, ignoring her resistance.

Or maybe it was because she didn't resist very much.

Rachel was exhausted. It had been a roller coaster of a day, up and down, and down and down, and even though she didn't want to care for him, she did. Her love wasn't a flimsy thing, but strong and deep and true.

"You have hurt me so much today," she whispered as he pulled her against him. She rested her cheek on his chest, his arm tight around her.

"I am sorry. I didn't want to bring those letters to you before the wedding, but how could I share them with you after?" He stroked her hair, and then down her back. "That would have been even worse. And so even though the timing was awful, I did what I thought was right. Shared with you everything I knew."

"Even though it meant ruining our day."

"I'd rather we ruin a day than start our marriage with a lie."

Rachel closed her eyes and breathed him in, needing his arms right now, and his warmth. She needed him and loved him, for better or worse. "And what would you do with me on our honeymoon?"

"I would make love to you three or four times a day. I would love you until you felt secure and understood that you're the only woman I have ever wanted to marry. I did not marry you out of obligation or to satisfy the international stock market."

She tipped her head back to look up at him. His bright blue eyes glinted with tenderness and humor.

"It's true," he added, his expression changing, the laughter giving way to a focused intensity. "I married you, *bella*, because I love you. And just in case you need to hear it again, Rachel, *bella, ti amo*. I love you. *I love you*. Do you understand?"

Her heart was beating a mile a minute. "I think so."

"You're not convinced?"

"Not entirely. Not yet."

"What else can I do?"

She touched her tongue to her upper lip, dampening it. "Take me on that honeymoon?"

He grinned, and then his grin faded and he

kissed her, a long, searing, bone-melting kiss. "We leave tomorrow," he said. "And we'd better sort out our birth control, or you'll be pregnant before you know it."

EPILOGUE

One year later

IT WAS LATE March and their first anniversary was just a week away. They were scheduled to leave for Ravello in two days to celebrate their first anniversary in style and enjoy a second honeymoon, something both Rachel and Gio were very much looking forward to.

But nothing was going to plan.

Again.

Instead of packing for their seaside villa in Ravello and anticipating their luxurious getaway in the glorious Italian sun, they were zipping along in the Marcello speedboat, heading to the hospital with Rachel tightly, frantically gripping Gio's hand.

She hurt. And she was scared. "He's coming too early," she gasped, as another swift, hard contraction hit.

Gio just held her hand until the contraction subsided. "We're almost to the hospital," he said quietly, leaning over to kiss her. "It won't be long now."

"But what is his hurry?" she cried, looking up into Gio's blue eyes. "He had another month to just hang out and relax. That was all he had to do, too."

Gio's lips quirked, and yet his touch was gentle and calming as he stroked her hair back from her damp brow. "I think he's eager to meet everybody and begin playing with his big brother."

"Well, he should have consulted me about his plans, because *I'm* not ready." Rachel gulped in another breath of air. "But just like a Marcello, he does what he wants and expects everyone to adjust and accommodate his whims."

Gio laughed softly. "Thank goodness you understand your Marcellos."

"You're all a lot of work!"

"And now you'll have one more."

Her tense expression eased, her lips curving. "Thank goodness I love little boys." She looked up into her husband's eyes. "I just want him healthy. I'm scared that he's coming too soon."

"Not all babies go full-term. I was early. He'll be perfect. I promise."

"He doesn't have to be perfect. I will love him however he is."

"I know you will. You are the best mother, the best wife." Gio kissed her again. *"Bella Rachel, ti amo."*

She blinked back tears. "I love you, too." She gripped his hand tighter. "I think the next contraction is starting. They're coming faster and closer." She blinked and exhaled, trying to remember her breathing, trying not to panic. "Oh, I just want to get there. I really don't want to give birth in a motorboat."

He leaned over, kissed her forehead. "We're almost there."

She clenched his hand hard as the contraction made everything tighten. "Oh—oh, Gio. This is serious."

The boat was slowing, the lights of the mainland ahead of them. "I see the ambulance," he said. "We're here. You're going to be fine."

"I don't know if *fine* is the word," she panted, "but as long as I'm not delivering in a speedboat, I won't complain. You know I love Venice, but this is a bit much."

He smiled at her, but didn't answer, too intent on helping her breathe through the pain. "I love you," he whispered as the contraction eased. "And I'm so proud of you. Together we have created the most extraordinary life."

Gio repeated the very same words less than an hour later as he held his newborn son, a boy they'd already decided to name Antonio after Gio's beloved brother.

Rachel blinked back tears as she watched Giovanni walk around her hospital room, cradling their son, murmuring to their newborn in Italian.

She still wasn't fluent in Italian but she understood what he was saying to baby Antonio.

I love you, my beautiful boy.

Her eyes stung all over again, her heart so very full.

They'd come full circle, she thought, and what an astonishing circle it was. Full of love and hope and the happy-ever-after she'd thought was only found in fairy tales.

Which must mean fairy tales did come true. At least, in Venice they did.

* * * * *

If you enjoyed
HIS MERCILESS MARRIAGE BARGAIN
by Jane Porter, you're sure to enjoy these other
CONVENIENTLY WED! *stories...*

BOUGHT WITH THE ITALIAN'S RING
by Tara Pammi
BOUND TO THE SICILIAN'S BED
by Sharon Kendrick
IMPRISONED BY THE GREEK'S RING
by Caitlin Crews

Coming soon!